KU-676-887

BRADY'S LAW

BRADY'S LAW

by

Wayne Gamble

Dales Large Print Books
Long Preston, North Yorkshire,
BD23 4ND, England.

DONCASTER LIBRARY AND
INFORMATION SERVICE

017872967

M   0 8 MAY 2001

LP   £10-99

British Library Cataloguing in Publication

Gamble, Wayne
Brady's law.

A catalogue record of this book is
available from the British Library

ISBN   1-84262-112-2 pbk

First published in Great Britain 1995 by Robert Hale Ltd.

Copyright © Wayne Gamble 1995

Cover illustration © Faba by arrangement with
Norma Editorial S.A.

The right of Wayne Gamble to be identified as the author of this
work has been asserted by him in accordance with the
Copyright, Designs and Patents Act, 1988

Published in Large Print 2001 by arrangement with
Robert Hale Ltd.

All Rights reserved. No part of this publication may be
reproduced, stored in a retrieval system, or transmitted in any
form or by any means, electronic, mechanical, photocopying,
recording or otherwise without the prior permission of the
Copyright owner.

Dales Large Print is an imprint of Library Magna Books Ltd.

Printed and bound in Great Britain by
T.J. (International) Ltd., Cornwall, PL28 8RW

R.C.

ONE

The two riders sat watching the thin spiral of smoke that was rising from the distant camp-fire. Both men were gazing intently at it through the early morning mist as if trying to read a message in the lazy wisp of smoke. The older of the two men, Tate Sharp, sat quietly as he waited for his younger companion to answer the question he had asked him several seconds earlier.

Tate was in his early sixties, and stood around five foot six inches tall. His rugged weather-beaten face and portly figure gave him a harmless fatherly appearance – an impression that had been the downfall of many an outlaw who had come up against the wily old bounty-hunter.

His companion's name was Sam Brady, and at seventeen years of age he still had that fresh clean-cut look of youth about him. He stood at six foot two inches tall, and had the gangling clumsy manner of a boy in a man's body, but his movements were fluid and deadly when it came to drawing and using the low-slung six-gun that was strapped to his right thigh.

Tate turned his gaze onto his young companion. 'Well, what do you think?' he prompted.

A frown creased Sam's brow as he made to answer. 'It seems all right to me. I can't see anything unusual over there,' he replied.

'You won't always see things with your eyes, Sam,' Tate explained patiently. 'You've got to learn to trust your natural senses and act by them. Don't you feel something unsettling in your gut about that campsite?'

Sam's frown deepened as he tried to analyse his inner feelings. He did feel a certain uneasiness, but he had put this down more to the hazy mist that they had been riding through for the past hour rather than anything to do with the distant campsite. Unable to honestly answer his companion's question, he shook his head dolefully.

Tate chuckled at seeing the troubled expression that played on the youngster's face. 'Come on, let's go over and check it out,' he directed.

Kneeing their horses into a walk, they closed in on the campsite. As they drew nearer they could clearly make out a large box-wagon parked amongst a stand of trees, and the unmistakable shape of a dead horse lying nearby. They could also see the huddled form of a person lying on the ground near the smouldering camp-fire.

On a signal from Tate, Sam pulled his horse to a halt and tugged his rifle from its boot. After checking its load, the youngster sat in watchful readiness while his older companion continued on towards the campsite.

Tate stopped his horse just short of the campsite and surveyed the scene around him. The person who was lying motionless on the ground near the camp-fire was completely covered by a blanket, with only their boots showing out from under one end. On moving his gaze to the horse that was lying on the ground near the wagon, he estimated that it had been dead for some time as it was already starting to bloat. The box-wagon itself was a common type used by drummers and medicine show men, and this one had the words 'SAINSBURY'S MERCHANDISE' painted on its side.

Swinging down from the saddle, the old bounty-hunter palmed his six-gun and walked over to the camp-fire. He nudged the huddled figure cautiously with his boot, but after getting no response he knelt down

9

and pulled back the blanket. The man who lay beneath it was in his late fifties, and had white shoulder-length hair and beard. At first Tate thought that the man was dead, but on touching his pallid skin he found it to be still warm and realized that he was either unconscious or in a deep sleep. This question was soon answered when he pulled the blanket back even further and saw the blood that was soaking the front of the man's shirt. A low whistle escaped the old bounty-hunter's lips as he wondered how this man could still be alive after losing so much blood.

After warily surveying the area once again, Tate gave his young companion the all-clear, and then waited for him to join him.

'Get my water-canteen, and some clean bandages out of my saddle-bags,' he instructed the youngster, before rolling the unconscious man over onto his back and unbuttoning his blood-soaked shirt. The old bounty-hunter shook his head in amazement when he pulled the man's shirt open to find two bullet-holes in the middle of his chest. On assuming that this shooting had happened around the same time that the horse had been shot, Tate wondered at just how he had managed to survive for so long.

'Is he still alive?' Sam asked as he knelt down beside his companion and surveyed the bloodied mess of the man's clothing.

'Yes, but only just,' the old bounty-hunter replied as he took the water-canteen and cloth, and then set about cleaning some of the blood from the man's chest.

'I'll take a look around,' Sam suggested as he climbed back to his feet.

'Okay, but be careful,' Tate warned, and briefly watched his young sidekick's cautious progress towards the wagon before turning his attention back to his patient. The old bounty-hunter realized that there was very little he could do to help him – and that it was only a matter of time before he would die from his wounds.

The sound of his young companion rattling the latch on the rear door of the box-wagon drew Tate's attention just as the deafening roar of a shotgun sounded out. The blast tore a large hole in the centre of the door, causing Sam to fall backwards to the ground in an untidy heap. Tate quickly pulled his six-gun from its holster and dived full length to the ground facing the wagon.

'Sam! Are you all right?' he asked, fearing that his young companion had been hit by the blast.

'Yes,' Sam answered unsteadily before crawling into the cover of a nearby tree. Luckily he had been standing off to one side of the wagon door when he tried the latch, so the shotgun blast had missed him completely.

'Did you get a look at the gunman?' Tate inquired.

The youngster took a deep breath to steady his jangled nerves before answering in a shaky voice. 'No – but I can assure you they are still in there.'

At that moment the wounded man groaned weakly and fixed Tate with a quizzical stare. His pale-blue eyes showed the pain that he was feeling as he tried to gather enough strength to speak.

'Hold on there a moment, mister – I've got to make sure that my young partner's safe before we can chinwag,' Tate interrupted him. 'Sam – keep the wagon covered while I see if our friend here knows who's in there with that shotgun.'

After receiving a nod from Sam in reply, the old bounty-hunter turned his attention back to the wounded man. 'Do you know who is in the wagon?'

'Y-yes,' the man groaned. 'It's my daughter... Please don't hurt her.'

'We won't if we can possibly avoid it,' Tate promised as he moved closer to the man's side. 'What's been going on around here?'

The man took several quick rasping breaths and closed his eyes tightly for several seconds before answering in a painful whisper. 'We set up camp yesterday afternoon intending to spend the night. Just after dark four men rode in – so we invited them to share our camp-fire and supper. After they had eaten they began drinking whiskey, and one of them grabbed hold of my daughter Sarah when she was collecting their meal-plates. I pulled him away from her and demanded that they leave our camp immediately, but he merely laughed in my face and pushed me aside before grabbing her again.'

Pity clutched at Tate's heart as he guessed at what had happened next. 'It's all right, friend,' Tate comforted the wounded man in an attempt to save him from further pain. 'You're safe with us now, so you can rest easy.'

Seeming not to hear these words, the man continued on in a hoarse whisper. 'My God... She is only sixteen years old, and that filthy animal hurt her so bad. When I tried to pull him away a second time he turned

13

and punched me, and then drew his gun and shot me. I can still hear Sarah begging me to help her as he dragged her away into the wagon – but I was hurt too bad to do anything.'

Tate reached out and took the wounded man's hand in his own, unable to find the words to comfort him.

'I begged his friends to stop him, but they just ignored me and kept on drinking. When he'd finished with her he came out and told them to mount up because he wanted to make it to Mitchell Wells before midnight, and as he rode out he shot our horse so we couldn't go for help.'

'Did you get these men's names?' Tate asked.

'Yes, and I'll never forget them,' the man rasped. 'The one who hurt Sarah introduced himself as Tyler Hobden, and the others as Vance Felton, Wilby Dixan and Ray Vidler.'

Tate shook his head sadly. These were the same men that he and Sam had been trailing for the past two weeks. All four of them were wanted for bank robbery and murder in several states, and they had big rewards on their heads.

'I'm dying, aren't I?' the man asked

bluntly, and after getting a nod in reply from Tate, he continued. 'Please look after Sarah for me. I'm her only family – so she has no-one else to turn to for help.'

'I'll look after her like my own daughter,' Tate assured him. 'And I also promise you that these men will pay for what they have done to you and your daughter.'

The man smiled his gratitude and squeezed Tate's hand warmly before slowly closing his eyes. It was as if he had fallen asleep again, but when Tate couldn't find any sign of a heartbeat he realized that the man had died.

TWO

Tate waited for Sam to join him out of earshot of the girl inside the wagon. He had already formulated a plan to disarm the girl, but its success would depend on the supple body and quick reflexes of his young companion.

'Who's in the wagon with the shotgun?' Sam asked as he stopped beside the old bounty-hunter.

15

'Her name is Sarah Sainsbury, and she's his daughter,' Tate explained, pointing at the dead man. 'She probably thought that we were Hobden and his men returning for her. It was him who shot her pa and very likely raped her as well – so I guess she has good reason to hate strange men at the moment.'

Sam felt a pang of guilt as he remembered the hostile thoughts he had directed at the person inside the wagon, but he now conceded that the girl had every cause to take a shot at the first strange male to come near her. An intense hatred for Tyler Hobden and his men grew inside him as he thought about what they had done to this girl and her father.

'What are we going to do now?' he asked.

The old bounty-hunter had already decided that there was very little hope of convincing the girl to come out of the wagon without a fight, so this meant that they would have to disarm her against her will.

'We've got to try to get that gun away from her,' he explained. 'I've got a plan worked out, but it'll depend on just how quick you are at grabbing her when I attract her attention at the rear door of the wagon.'

Sam eyed Tate warily. 'She's already tried to blow my head off once, and now you want me to give her another go at it?'

'I'll be the one that she will be pointing the gun at,' Tate explained patiently. 'Your job will be to jump in through that little hatchway behind the driver's seat and simply grab her.'

'Your plans always sound simple but they usually end up with me being on the receiving end,' Sam grumbled before moving off towards the wagon.

Tate smiled to himself as he watched his young partner walk away. They had been together for nearly a year now, and it amused him to see how Sam's self-confidence had grown to the point where he now no longer mutely accepted everything that Tate said – and in fact at times he often showed signs of downright rebellion in his responses.

After searching around and finding a stick suitable for his part in the plan, Tate moved over to the side of the wagon near the rear door and waited while Sam climbed up onto the front of the wagon and settled into position on the driver's seat. The old bounty-hunter then tied a piece of rag on the end of the stick and waved it in front of the hole in the door left by the previous shotgun blast. Almost immediately the shotgun crashed out again, tearing the rag to shreds and splintering the end of the stick.

Sam instantly launched himself in through the hatchway, but managed to get the curtain that hung over the opening caught around his head and shoulders in the process. He crashed to the floor of the wagon and tore wildly at the cloth that obscured his vision, expecting any moment to feel the impact of shotgun pellets as they tore through his body.

A voice to Sam's left cried out as he finally dislodged the curtain and sprang to his feet, but once again darkness clouded his vision when the shotgun barrel struck him solidly across the side of his head. In a frantic attempt to gain time to allow his senses to recover, he lunged at the girl and wrapped his arms around her tightly.

She fought like a wildcat in his grasp and dropped the shotgun noisily to the floor as she attempted to get her hands free to inflict as much damage as possible to her sup-posed attacker. Quickly regaining his senses, he hugged her to his chest even more tightly to prevent her from reaching his face with her hands. Changing her point of attack, she kicked at his shins and pulled at his hair in

an attempt to force him to break his grip –
but her energy quickly dissipated and she
gave out a heart-rending cry before col-
lapsing unconscious into his arms.

Sam stood for a moment still dazed by the
furious fight that she had put up. Relaxing
his grip from around her small body, he
lifted her into his arms and carried her
across to lay her on the bunk positioned
against the side wall. He then sat down
beside her and gazed in awe at her angelic
face.

'Are you okay, Sam?' Tate asked anxiously
from outside the wagon.

'Yes,' the youngster replied. 'You can come
in now.'

Tate opened the door and climbed the
steps up into the wagon. 'I thought she must
have got you,' he smiled as he moved up
next to his young partner, but the smile died
on the old bounty-hunter's face when he
saw the frail young girl lying on the bunk.
He gazed in wonder at her ivory-white skin
and long blonde hair that gave her a
wondrous beauty, but loathing for Hobden
and his men grew inside him when he saw
her torn clothing and bruised face. Her
slight build was more like that of a twelve-
year-old child than of a sixteen-year-old,

19

and Tate wondered what kind of man could possibly hurt such a beautiful young girl.

'What'll happen to her now?' Sam asked sadly, finding it impossible to move his gaze from her face.

'We'll take her to stay with a couple I know who live about eight miles from here. They will take care of her until we've dealt with Hobden and his men, and then I'll work out something more permanent for her.'

'What about her family or relatives?' Sam asked.

Tate shook his head sadly. 'Her father told me before he died that she had no other family, and he begged me to take care of her,' he explained.

Sam nodded his understanding, but found it impossible to imagine what it would be like to have no family. His own family lived on a small ranch just outside the town of Alstonville in Southern Kansas. It was nearing twelve months now since he had packed his saddle-bags and ridden out after a heated argument with his father, Dan Brady. His father was a quiet man and very hard to anger, but Sam's constant practising with his six-gun and subsequent neglect of ranch duties had finally brought them into open conflict. Sam had met up with Tate Sharp on a lonely trail leading into Texas within a week of leaving his family home, and the two had shared a campfire for the night and struck up an instant friendship. The next day the youngster had readily accepted the old bounty-hunter's offer to become partners in the deadly trade of hunting bounty, and after eleven months riding together they still enjoyed a strong friendship.

Tate had been told by his young partner the reason why he had left home in the first place – and had often tried to persuade him to write home to his parents to ease their minds, but to date he had resisted this advice. Unknown to Sam, Tate had written to Dan and Katherine Brady some six months before to assure them that their son was safe and well, and that given time he was sure that Sam would contact them himself.

As Sam sat looking at the unconscious girl he began to think about his family and how much he missed them. This girl had no-one to turn to for help and now had to depend on strangers to care for her. Emotion welled up in his chest as he silently vowed to pro-tect her from any further harm, and to avenge the hurt that she had suffered at the hands of Tyler Hobden.

Tate called Sam to join him outside the wagon, where they wrapped the girl's father's body in a blanket before carrying it inside and tying it onto the second bunk. Sam then stayed with the unconscious girl while Tate went out to harness his own horse to the wagon.

It wasn't long before the wagon lurched into motion and they started off along the trail towards Mitchell Wells.

THREE

Sarah Sainsbury stood looking up at her father. He was seated on a large white stallion and was smiling down at her in his usual loving way. She reached out to touch his leg, but the stallion shied away and pranced off several yards before stopping again. Suddenly she realized that her father had no control over the horse, and that it had no saddle or bridle.

'Please get off him, Father. He might hurt you,' she begged, knowing that he was never a good horseman.

'It's okay, Sarah,' he assured her lovingly. 'He can't hurt me.'

The horse pranced away several more yards when she made to walk towards it. 'Please, Father. I think you should get off him before he throws you.'

Her father merely smiled and waved to her as the big stallion began a dancing walk away into the swirling mist.

'Father, don't leave me,' she cried.

'You'll be all right, Sarah,' he assured her as he moved further off into the mist. 'They will look after you.'

'Who will look after me?' she asked anxiously, but his answer was too muffled for her to hear because he'd moved too far off into the swirling mist.

On noticing the confused expression on his daughter's face, he pointed off to her left where there were two men walking towards her out of the mist. The one in front smiled at her, but his hard cruel eyes showed no kindness.

Suddenly Sarah recognized him as the man who had shot her father, and defiled her body. She screamed out loud as panic exploded inside her, and she turned and tried to run off after her father but the man grabbed her by the wrist and held her. She screamed loudly once again and tried to break free of his iron-like grasp – but he was too strong for her.

'Don't leave me with them,' she begged, but her father was now completely out of sight in the mist.

'You're all mine now, you sweet young thing,' the man leered, and used his superior strength to force her down onto her back on the ground.

'Nnnn-no!' she screamed out, and struggled vainly in his grasp as he pinned her arms to the ground. Racking sobs shook her body as she felt her strength beginning to fade, and she realized that there was no escaping this man. She closed her eyes tightly and prayed for death to take her before this man could hurt her again.

A gentle reassuring voice slowly penetrated her terror-stricken mind, but she tried to ignore it knowing that it was only the loathsome man trying to trick her. The voice continued on in the same gentle reassuring manner, and slowly her sobbing subsided and she became aware of the ground moving around beneath her.

Slowly, Sarah opened her eyes and looked straight into the face of a handsome young man with soft brown eyes and long blond hair. It confused her to see the tears that were plainly evident in his eyes and the look of concern written on his face.

'I'm not going to hurt you,' he promised emotionally.

Realizing that he had her arms pinned to the bed, she began to struggle in his grasp. 'Please let me go,' she begged him.

Sam hesitantly released his grip and sat back to watch the girl push herself up into a sitting position, and then cower back away from him into the corner like a frightened animal.

'I promise I won't hurt you,' he assured her.

'Where's my father?' she asked timidly.

Sam hesitated as he tried to decide whether to lie to her or to tell her the truth about her father, but settled on the latter. 'He died this morning just after we found your camp,' he confessed.

'You're lying!' she accused angrily without taking her eyes from his face. 'Where are you taking me, and what have you done with my father?'

'We're taking you to a family who live nearby – and I am telling you the truth about your father. By the time we came across your campsite it was too late to help him.'

Memories of the previous night flooded back into her mind and she realized that he was telling the truth. She began sobbing quietly as grief tore at her heart, and this drained away the last of her frail energy supply. Sleep once again closed in on her, and she went willingly when she felt Sam take her into his arms and hold her tightly against his chest as she drifted off – feeling safe under his protection.

FOUR

Hobden waited patiently in the alleyway for the signal that he was to receive from one of his men when his quarry was in sight. It was nearing eight o'clock in the morning and he was finding he was having trouble keeping his mind on the job at hand. He and his men had arrived in town late the previous evening, and that along with their early start that morning was having an effect on his alertness. The sound of someone whistling drew his attention, and the outlaw leader looked up to see Ray Vidler standing across the street leaning against a wooden post at the front of a shop. Taking this as his cue, Hobden moved off towards the alley-mouth where he waited with his six-gun ready in his hand.

Within seconds a man came into view as he crossed the mouth of the alley, and Hobden stepped out behind him and pushed the muzzle of his six-gun into his back.

'Keep walking straight ahead, and keep your mouth shut or you're a dead man,' the outlaw leader warned.

Walter Brown was the manager of the local bank. He was a short fat man with a balding pate, and was wearing an ill-fitting light-grey suit. He stiffened noticeably on hearing Hobden's directive, but his stride didn't falter as he continued along the street.

'Stop at the front door of the bank and open up the way you usually do – and please don't make me kill you by trying to play the hero,' Hobden cautioned him.

Brown silently did as he was bid. This was the third time in five years that he had been held up, and he had decided long ago that he enjoyed life too much to throw it away over someone else's money. The two men stopped at the front door of the bank, and the bank manager pulled his keys from his vest pocket and inserted one into the door-lock.

Hobden took the moment to look back over his shoulder and signal Ray Vidler, who instantly left his position and headed across the street for the alleyway that ran along the side of the bank building.

'Hurry up,' Hobden growled, and pushed the muzzle of his six-gun into Brown's kidney for good measure.

The door swung back on its hinges, and Hobden pushed the bank manager roughly through the door so that he too could move inside. 'Now move through to the back door and open it,' he instructed Brown.

The bank manager did as he was bid, and soon Ray Vidler and Vance Felton had joined their leader inside the bank.

'You cover the door, Vance – while Ray and me help our friend here to open the safe,' Hobden directed, and waited until his order was carried out before turning back to Brown. 'Open the safe and don't mess around doing it.'

'I-I can't,' the bank manager stammered with beads of sweat glistening on his brow. 'It needs two keys and I only carry one of them.'

Hobden merely shrugged his shoulders and seemed totally unconcerned about this news. 'I was told that you'd have both of the keys, Wally – but we've come prepared just in case something like this happened. Give me the dynamite, Ray,' he demanded, and watched as his companion opened a small shoulder-bag and pulled out a bundle of explosives that had a fuse protruding from one end.

'Seeing that you're not going to help us, Wally – you're going to be tied up next to your precious safe when this lot goes off,' Hobden snarled. 'Now move over there so we can tie you up.'

'Nnn-no!' the banker screamed. 'I'd like to be able to help you but I only have the one key.'

'That is your bad luck,' the outlaw leader declared as he pulled back the hammer on his six-gun and aimed it at Brown's head. 'Now do as I bid or die where you stand.'

'There is a spare second key,' the bank manager moaned as he looked into the black hole that was the muzzle of the outlaw leader's six-gun. 'It's kept in the top drawer of the desk over in the corner.'

'Get it,' Hobden demanded, and he then waited while the bank manager crossed to the desk and used his keys to open the drawer. Brown quickly found the second key and passed it across to the outlaw leader.

'Open the safe, Ray,' Hobden ordered his companion, who took both of the keys and crossed the room to the large iron safe that was built into the wall behind the counter.

There were two loud clicking sounds as both keys turned easily in their locks, and the outlaw swung the large iron door open to reveal a considerable amount of money stacked in neat piles on the shelves.

'Leave the coins and only take paper money,' the outlaw leader instructed his companion as he threw several empty cotton sacks over to him.

'I know my job – I'm not stupid,' Vidler growled as he picked the sacks up from the floor.

'Just do as you're told, and button your lip,' Hobden warned his companion in return. 'Or maybe you'd like to stay behind when we leave?'

Ray Vidler didn't bother to respond to this threat, but he seethed with anger at having to give ground. He wasn't scared of Hobden, but he realized that the outlaw leader was quite capable of carrying out his threat. This along with the fact that life had never been as good as it had been since he threw in with Hobden convinced him to shut his mouth and quietly fill the sacks as instructed.

'Someone's coming,' Vance Felton warned

from his lookout position at the front door. 'And he is heading straight for the bank.'

'It'll be young Scott Langley – one of my tellers,' the bank manager explained hurriedly. 'He's only a kid, so please don't hurt him.'

'Open the door as soon as he stops outside, and let him in before he can suspect anything,' Hobden directed as he too moved over to stand near the main doorway.

Vance Felton nodded his head and continued to watch the approaching youngster through a gap in the curtains.

'He's here,' he announced, and he reached out and pulled the door open to allow the young teller to enter.

Scott Langley stepped into the room with a bright smile on his face, but this turned to a frown as he took in the scene of the man emptying the contents of the safe into a white cotton sack. 'What in the devil's name...?' he began to ask, but got no further as Hobden viciously pistol-whipped him across the back of his head, knocking him unconscious.

'You didn't have to do that,' Walter Brown objected as he moved across the room to where the youngster lay in a heap on the floor.

'Give old Wally here a hand to drag him around behind the counter, and then get back to your position at the door,' Hobden directed Vance Felton.

'Come on, Ray – haven't you finished yet?' he continued testily, but at that moment his companion was tying off the last sack.

'I'm ready when you are,' Vidler answered as he climbed to his feet and slung the four full sacks of money over his shoulder.

'Right,' Hobden grinned. 'Move over here and wait with Vance near the door. Wilby should be here any minute with the horses.'

Vidler did as he was directed and moved across to stand next to Felton, while Hobden turned his attention back to the bank manager, who was kneeling behind the counter next to his unconscious teller.

'You lie down on the floor next to the youngster and don't move until we are well clear of town – that is if you want to stay alive,' the outlaw warned.

Brown lowered himself onto his hands and knees, and then lay down on his stomach with his head resting on his arms, and made no attempt to look up as Hobden crossed the room to stand with his two companions at the front door.

'Here comes Wilby with the horses,' Vance

Felton stated. 'And the street looks clear of people at the moment.'

Tyler Hobden smiled. 'You two make for the horses when I give the word, and cover me if anyone starts shooting. I'll bring these along with me just to make sure that you don't decide to leave me behind,' he declared as he took the sacks of money from Ray Vidler and hung them over his own shoulder. Neither of his companions argued with him as it was common for Hobden to do this whenever they had scored a large haul of cash like this.

'Wilby's now in position,' Felton announced.

The outlaw leader pulled a match from his pocket and lit the fuse that was sticking out of the end of the bundle of dynamite. He watched the fuse splutter into life and then burn furiously, before turning to his companions.

'Go now,' he directed.

Both men stepped out through the door and walked across to their horses. Hobden watched their progress and waited until they were in their saddles before he made ready for his own escape. He tossed the bundled dynamite over the counter before hurrying out of the bank and climbing up onto his horse. There was a deafening roar as the front windows of the bank disintegrated, and all the outlaws' horses reared and kicked in fright from the noise.

A maniacal laugh escaped Hobden as he brought his horse back under control and spurred it into a run along the street. 'That'll keep them busy for a while,' he shouted across to his companions as they sped out of town without one shot being fired at them.

FIVE

Sam stood quietly and watched as Tate and his companion shovelled dirt into the grave that contained the body of Sarah's father. They were standing some fifty yards from the house under the shade of a tree, and the youngster was feeling frustrated at not being on Hobden's trail.

On their arrival at the Ward farm they had been warmly greeted by Tate's old friends. Bob Ward was a giant of a man who stood around six foot six inches tall. His face was covered with a heavy black beard that hung halfway down his chest, but his blue eyes and easy smile gave him an air of gentleness. His wife, Hope, was the complete opposite to him. She stood around five foot two inches tall, and had a petite build that reminded Sam of a small china doll he had once seen in a shop, but her flaming red hair warned that she would have a temper to be avoided at all costs. On hearing of the assault on Sarah Sainsbury, Hope had taken charge and had the still-unconscious girl carried into the house. That had been forty minutes earlier and in the meantime the men had kept themselves busy by digging a grave and burying Sarah's father's body.

The old bounty-hunter and Bob Ward finally stood back from the grave and surveyed their spadework.

'Come on, Tate, let's get our horses and get out after Hobden and his men,' Sam growled as his patience finally gave out, and he then turned and headed for his horse.

Bob Ward watched as Tate hurried off after the youngster and caught up with him half-way between the house and the grave site.

'Listen to me, young man,' he demanded as he grabbed Sam by the arm and halted his progress. 'We've been together for just on eleven months now, and up until now you have shown an ability to think before you acted. Well, you had better slow down a bit right now and try thinking this one through before you go running off half-cocked and end up with your head blown off.'

Sam locked eyes with Tate and for a moment looked as if he was going to argue, but instead took a deep breath and released his pent-up frustration with an explosive sigh.

'You're right, Tate,' he admitted finally. 'It's just that I can't seem to get what those animals did to Sarah out of my mind.'

A sad smile creased Tate's face. 'You're not the only one to feel angry about this, Sam,' he assured his young companion. 'But if we go charging off after Hobden and his gang with nothing but revenge in our minds, we will end up like Sarah's father over there. We have to get ourselves organized and then we'll stick to their trail until we get them.'

Another deep sigh escaped Sam as he nodded his acceptance of his old partner's wisdom, and he was about to reply when he heard Hope calling out his name from the direction of the house.

'Let's go and see what she wants,' Tate suggested, and they walked off towards the house together.

'Sarah's awake and wants to speak to the young man with beautiful brown eyes and long blond hair,' she explained.

'You won't be seeing her again for some time, so you may as well go and say your goodbyes now,' Tate suggested, and then pulled a bundled neckerchief from his coat pocket and passed it across to him. 'Give these things to her while you're in there – they belonged to her father.'

Sam took the small bundle from Tate and walked off into the house. When he reached the bedroom he found the girl lying on the double bed with a blanket covering her to the neck, and he thought for a moment that she was asleep until she opened her eyes and looked directly at him. He felt his heart pound in his chest when he looked into her beautiful blue eyes, and they glistened like sapphires as she watched him cross the room and stop beside the bed.

'You wanted to see me?' he asked awkwardly.

A gentle smile eased her features as she looked up at his face. 'I just wanted to thank you for looking after me earlier today,' she confided in a quiet voice. 'And I'm sorry if I hurt you in any way.'

'You didn't hurt me,' Sam assured her

gently. 'I was more worried that I might have hurt you.'

The girl didn't bother to respond to this but instead shook her head sadly and smiled up at him.

Sam suddenly remembered the items that Tate had given him for her. 'These things belonged to your father,' he informed her as he hesitantly passed them across to her.

Sarah opened the bundled neckerchief and tears welled in her eyes as she viewed its contents. She sobbed quietly to herself as she touched each of the items in turn, and then finally picked out a silver half-hunter watch and passed it across to Sam.

'I want you to have that,' she announced in a voice that was choked with emotion. 'My mother gave it to my father on their last wedding anniversary before she died, and I'm sure he would be proud if you took it.'

Sam found it impossible to speak as he realized the significance of the gift. He turned the watch over in his hand and admired its finely engraved silver case, before finally finding his voice. 'Are you sure you want me to have this?' he asked.

'I'm positive,' she declared firmly.

'Thank you, Sarah,' he replied gratefully. 'And I will always treasure it because it will remind me of you.'

Sarah smiled shyly at his reply, and reached out and took his hand in her own before speaking. 'While-ever you carry that watch I will always be with you,' she vowed.

Now it was Sam's turn to feel embarrassed, and he tried to think of something to say in return, but it was the girl who spoke first. 'Hope told me that she has never met you before today, Sam – and she wasn't sure whether you were related to Tate or not?'

'No – I'm not related to Tate,' he informed her. 'I met up with him on the trail about eleven months back – and we've been riding together ever since.'

'Is your family still living?'

'Yes – and they live on a small ranch down in Southern Kansas. I've got a twin brother named Luke and a younger sister who is called Sarah the same as you.'

'You're a twin?' she asked in an incredulous voice.

'Yes – an identical twin,' he replied with a smile on his face. 'Although, I always thought I was the better-looking one out of the two of us.'

Sarah frowned as she tried to comprehend how he could be better-looking than his identical twin brother, but this frown turned to a smile when she saw him grinning impishly at her. 'You're teasing me,' she accused him. 'Go on and tell me more about your family in Kansas.'

The two continued to talk easily for some time, and it wasn't until Sam let slip that he hadn't written to his parents since leaving home that a frown once more knitted her brow. 'You must write to your parents and let them know that you are all right, Sam,' she declared. 'What must they be thinking has happened to you? They'll be worrying themselves sick.'

A feeling of guilt settled on Sam and he didn't know how to answer her criticism. He had often tried to write to his mother to let her know that he was all right, but the angry words that had passed between himself and his father always came back into his mind and this seemed to push the thought of writing a letter from his mind. But this was the first time he had thought about the effect that his disappearance would be having on his family, and he now realized that he had been foolish to allow his pride to override his duty to his family.

'I promise you that I'll write to them as soon as I get back from dealing with Tyler Hobden,' he assured her, and instantly regretted mentioning the outlaw leader's name.

Tears once again formed in Sarah's eyes and she turned her head aside to hide this from him, but the momentary spell of happiness that they had shared was now broken. The energy consumed by her grief quickly tired her, and she drifted off into a deep sleep that once again freed her tortured mind.

Sam reached out and touched her cheek with his fingers as if making certain that she was real. His heart once again swelled in his chest as he remembered what she had been put through the previous night. 'I promise you on my life that Hobden and his men will pay dearly for what they have done to you,' he vowed before slipping the watch into his breast pocket and leaving the room.

SIX

The three horse-riders rode along side by side as they closed in on the town of Mitchell Wells. Sam was flanked by Tate Sharp on one side and Bob Ward on the other, and he had hardly spoken a word to either since leaving Sarah Sainsbury back at the farmhouse. His two companions had wisely left him to his thoughts, as they both realized how much the youngster had taken the violation of the girl by Tyler Hobden to heart.

It had surprised Sam to find Bob Ward mounted on his horse and waiting with Tate when he had walked out of the house, but he had assumed that the farmer had decided to ride with them into town.

The three men slowed their mounts as they entered the outskirts of Mitchell Wells. It was a medium-sized town whose main purpose was to provide the commercial goods and financial services required by the surrounding farms. The streets were strangely deserted, and Sam looked across at Tate, who also seemed to have noticed this.

'If we see Hobden and his men we must keep clear of them until we've had a chance to speak to the local law,' Tate warned his young companion.

'You do that,' Sam answered rebelliously. He found it impossible to push the memory of Sarah crying herself to sleep from his mind, and this served to intensify the hatred he was feeling for Hobden and his men.

Tate was about to insist that his young companion do as he was bid, but realized that it might have the effect of causing Sam to head off on his own after Hobden and his men in an attempt to effect his revenge on them. Instead, the old bounty-hunter decided to bide his time and face up to each situation as it occurred, and hopefully guide Sam away from any danger.

They were now approaching the centre of the town and could plainly see the damage done to the front of the bank from the explosion set by Hobden. There were still quite a few people milling around the front of the building, and the three riders stopped their horses to view the damage.

'What happened here, Jake?' Bob Ward asked an old man who was standing at the horse-rail.

'Someone knocked the bank over, and killed Walter Brown and one of his young tellers,' he explained.

'Now we know why Hobden and his men were in such a hurry to reach Mitchell Wells last night,' Tate declared before directing a question at the old-timer. 'I guess the sheriff is out of town on their trail?'

'Yep – sure is. He headed out of town with a twenty-man posse about an hour and a half ago, but his deputy's still around here somewhere helping tidy things up,' he stated.

'Let's get out after them before they can cover their tracks,' Sam insisted impatiently.

'You go over to the saloon and wait for us while we go and chase up this deputy,' Tate instructed the youngster, and continued on after seeing the rebellious look in his eyes: 'I promise you we will get them, but you must trust me in this and let me do the planning.'

Once again biting back his impatience, Sam nodded his compliance with Tate's request and started his horse off along the street towards the saloon, while Tate and Bob dismounted and walked off towards the sheriff's office.

Sam pushed through the batwing doors of the saloon and crossed to the bar. He looked about him while he waited for the barman to reluctantly move along to where he was standing. The only other people in the bar-room were three men standing at the far end of the bar, and their main topic of conversation seemed to be the violent raid on the local bank that morning.

'What can I do for you, kid?' the barman asked irritably as he stopped in front of Sam.

'A beer please,' the youngster requested, ignoring the patronizing tone in the barman's voice.

'We don't serve kids in here,' the barman declared as he turned and made to walk back along to the other end of the bar so he could rejoin the conversation that Sam's arrival had interrupted.

'Hold it, mister,' Sam demanded coolly, and as the barman stopped the youngster laid his six-gun on the bar-top with the barrel pointing at him. 'I asked for a beer – I didn't ask for your smart-mouthed comments.'

The barman looked at the six-gun, and then at Sam's hand where it was resting on the bar-top within inches of the weapon. His own hand started to reach out towards the edge of the bar when a voice called out from the far end of the bar and stopped him.

'Hold it, Harold,' it demanded, and one of the men moved away from the group and walked towards Sam.

'You must really need that drink if you are willing to die for it, son,' the man surmised as he stopped and faced the young bounty-hunter. 'Harold here could have shot you dead and no court in this land would have blamed him after that little trick you pulled with your six-gun.'

Sam realized that the stranger was right, but the anger and hatred he was feeling for Hobden was having a marked effect on his reasoning. 'The way I see it, it's really got nothing to do with you, mister,' he replied coolly.

The stranger pulled back his jacket to expose a deputy sheriff's star pinned to his vest. 'I think it has a lot to do with me,' he replied equally as coolly. 'And it might be a good idea if you were to put that six-gun back in its holster, and leave the saloon quietly.'

Sam picked up his six-gun and slid it back into his low-slung holster. 'I came in here for a drink and I intend having one before I leave,' he declared stubbornly. 'And if the barman had gone for that scatter-gun that he keeps under the bar he would have ended up one dead hombre.'

'Harold has the right to serve or not serve whoever he wants,' the deputy sheriff informed him. 'So if you want to take this further I guess it will have to be sorted out between you and me.'

Easing back from the bar, Sam lowered his hand to his holstered six-gun. His face showed no emotion, and his stare was unwavering as he locked eyes with the deputy.

'If you insist on buying in on this you had better make ready to use that six-gun,' the youngster growled.

The deputy sheriff pulled his jacket back clear of his low-slung six-gun and waited for the youngster to make a move. His pale-blue eyes locked onto Sam's, and there was a faint twist of a smile on his lips. 'Make your move when you're ready,' he instructed.

'What the hell is going on here?' Tate Sharp demanded as he entered the barroom from the street. 'Don't either of you two dare touch those weapons until we've had a chance to sort this out.'

He quickly crossed the room and stopped between Sam and the deputy sheriff. 'How the hell can you get into so much trouble just waiting for me in a saloon?' he asked his young companion angrily.

'All I asked for was one drink, and they're the ones who decided to make an issue out of it,' the youngster replied unrepentantly.

Tate turned towards the deputy sheriff, and smiled as he recognized him. 'Hell – if it isn't Duke Baxter,' he declared, and reached out and shook hands with him. 'It's been many years since I saw you last.'

'It's been too long, Tate,' the deputy smiled broadly in return. 'Is this youngster with you?'

'Yes – but I'm starting to wonder if he's worth all the trouble,' the old bounty-hunter grumbled in return, before turning back to face his young companion. 'Hell's sake, Sam. You're going to end up as bad as Hobden himself if you're willing to shoot a man over a glass of beer.'

Sam's face flushed with shame as he realized that Tate was right. He had been prepared to fight and kill another man just to salve his own pride, and that did make him as bad as the lowest kind of human. He dropped his eyes to the floor and felt conscience-stricken as he searched for words to express his regret. 'I'm sorry, Tate. I guess I'm not myself at the moment,' he offered.

'If you don't start using that brain of yours soon, you will be dead sorry,' the old bounty-hunter lectured. 'You may never have heard of Duke Baxter, but he's the quickest gun you will ever see in your life – and you damn near found out the hard way.'

Sam looked past Tate and locked eyes with Baxter. The deputy sheriff gave him a broad wink and smiled at Sam to ease the tension of the dressing-down that he had just received from the old bounty-hunter.

'I'm really sorry to have pushed you, Mr Baxter,' Sam said with sincerity in his voice.

'Call me Duke,' Baxter smiled and offered the youngster his hand. 'I guess it was partly my fault too. Any man who needed a drink as badly as you shouldn't have been kept away from it. Harold, I think we can turn a blind eye to the rules just this once and give the youngster a drink along with a couple more for me and my good friend Tate here.'

The barman served the drinks, and the three men moved over to an empty table to talk. Sam sat silently while Tate and Duke talked freely about their past meetings and the friends they had in common.

'I heard you got yourself married and settled down in a town in Southern Arkansas?' Tate stated finally.

The deputy sheriff looked down at his drink and it took him several seconds before he answered. 'I was married, but I'm not any more.'

'It didn't work out for you, eh?' the old bounty-hunter prompted.

'Something like that,' he replied, and offered no more information before changing the subject. 'What brings you into this part of the country, Tate?'

The old bounty-hunter took the hint and moved on to the subject of Tyler Hobden and his men.

SEVEN

Duke Baxter waited on his horse next to Tate, Sam and Bob on a small rise in the trail and watched the returning posse close in on their position. The posse was riding in a broken formation with the sheriff in the lead, and they were leading three horses that carried bodies tied across their saddles. On reaching the deputy sheriff and his companions, the posse reined in to face them.

'Did you catch up with them?' Baxter inquired as he eyed the bodies tied to the horses.

'Yes,' the old sheriff growled irritably. 'And I lost three good men in the process.'

'Did you get any of the outlaws?' Tate asked.

'No,' the sheriff replied bitterly. 'They set up an ambush for us just this side of the state border, and we rode straight into the middle of it like a bunch of ducks in a shooting-gallery – and after shooting us up they then just hightailed it across the border.'

'Why didn't you go after them?' Sam asked impatiently.

The old sheriff eyed the youngster for a moment before finally answering. 'My authority as a lawman finishes at the state border, young man. That, along with the fact that I have already lost three good men made me curb my urge to chase them to hell and back, and think instead about these townsmen and their families.'

The young bounty-hunter dropped his eyes under the cool gaze of the old lawman, and he realized that he still wasn't using his brain to think things through before he opened his mouth.

'I've decided to ride out with these gents to look for Hobden and his men, and seeing we'll be crossing the state border I guess you'll want this back,' Baxter announced as he made to unclip his deputy's badge from his pocket.

'Take it with you,' the old sheriff directed. 'It won't give you any power over the border, but at least you will be representing the local community when you catch up with those cold-blooded killers.'

Baxter nodded his thanks and bid farewell to the sheriff and his possemen, before then starting his horse off along the trail – closely followed by his three companions.

The four men rode along at an easy canter to cover as much distance as possible, while at the same time allowing their horses to conserve their energy. Finally the group of hills that marked the state border came into view and they reined in their horses.

'We must keep our wits about us just in case Hobden is still waiting up in the hills,' Tate warned.

'Why do you think Hobden stopped and set that ambush for the posse?' Bob Ward asked curiously.

The old bounty-hunter thought about it for a moment before answering. 'Hobden's got a reputation for doing crazy things just for the fun of it. My guess is that he knew he was pretty safe by being so close to the state border, and decided to make sure that the posse didn't get too keen and pursue them any further.'

The four men then pushed on along the trail and soon came across the place where the posse had earlier been ambushed. The ground was strewn with bullet-shells where the posse had put up their fight, but there were no obvious signs of where the outlaws had been positioned when they fired down on the posse.

'I suggest that we push on for the border and hope that we pick up Hobden's tracks somewhere along the way,' Tate suggested to his companions.

'I agree,' Duke Baxter declared. 'I reckon they will be heading for the town of Logan to the north of here.'

'You might be right,' Tate mused. 'But I heard that one of Hobden's men comes from these parts, so they may well be heading there to hole up for a while.'

Further conversation was then put aside as they pushed on along the trail, and as they crossed the state border they picked up some horse-tracks that could only have belonged to Hobden and his men.

'If I know Hobden's mind he will have left some of his men behind him on the trail to make sure that the posse didn't decide to follow them after all,' Tate surmised. 'I think it would be a good idea if I went on ahead to see if I can draw them out before they spot you lot.'

'If any of his men are watching the trail up ahead they will suspect any rider travelling this close behind them as being part of the posse, and may well have a pot-shot at them just to make sure,' Bob Ward explained calmly.

'He's right, Tate,' Duke Baxter declared. 'We would be better off sticking together and facing the problem of an ambush if we come across it.'

A look of irritation crossed the old bounty-hunter's face as he considered the other two men's comments. He knew they were both right, but he also knew that it was very likely that at least two of his group would be hit before they would have a chance to react if they were to ride blindly into an ambush.

'I still think it'd be a better idea for me to ride on ahead and draw out any ambushers,' he insisted. 'I know they may well shoot first and ask questions later, but it's a better risk than all of us riding into an ambush.'

'I don't like the idea, but I guess you're right,' the deputy agreed reluctantly, and received a nod of assent from Bob Ward in support.

'There is one other option,' Sam revealed to his three companions, and continued on after receiving their full attention. 'No-one would suspect a kid like me of being a danger to them – even if I was armed.'

'No way, Sam!' Tate Sharp growled instantly.

'Hang on there a minute, Tate,' Duke Baxter challenged. 'It is a good idea, and young Sam is right when he says they wouldn't suspect him as being a danger to them.'

'I don't like the idea,' the old bounty-hunter insisted, but his main worry was whether the youngster would be able to keep his head if confronted by Hobden's men.

'Don't you think I'm capable, Tate?' Sam asked evenly.

The old bounty-hunter locked eyes with the youngster and was tempted to speak his mind, but realized that the plan was quite workable and that Sam was more than capable of carrying it off. 'Okay, but keep your eyes open and be damn careful,' he finally relented, and bit back the urge to give his young companion detailed instructions on how to carry out the plan.

A slow smile settled on the young bounty-hunter's face as he thanked Tate for backing him. He then assured his companions that he would do his best to signal them if he saw anyone – before then moving off along the trail alone.

The sun was just about directly overhead

as Sam pushed his mount along at an easy walk through the broken landscape. The heat of the sun began to parch his throat and after covering about four miles he decided to stop to drink some water. As he was about to lift the canteen to his lips he saw the glint of sunlight reflecting off something metallic in amongst the rocks further along the trail to his right, and when he saw movement in the same area he knew that he was being watched. So as not to let them know that he had seen them he continued to drink from his canteen, but he kept a watchful eye on the rocks for any further sign of movement.

Sam knew that he should wait for Tate and the others to catch up so they could help him to flush the ambusher out of his hiding-place, but the hatred he felt for Hobden and his men made this idea intolerable. Pushing his horse into a walk, the young bounty-hunter moved off along the trail once again. He kept his hands well clear of his weapons and whistled tunelessly out loud so as to give the impression to anyone watching him that he was in no hurry, and was of no danger to them. He was soon passing the spot where he had earlier seen movement amongst the rocks, but he still couldn't stop himself from being startled when a voice called out a challenge to him.

'Stop right there, kid – and put your hands in the air!'

Sam quickly reined in and raised his hands in the air as ordered. He then slowly turned his head to see a lone man standing between two rocks holding a rifle.

'There's no use holding me up, mister,' the young bounty-hunter stated. 'I've got no money, and my horse is just an old hack.'

'I don't want your horse or money, kid,' the gunman assured him. 'I want to know if you saw anyone else on the trail back there?'

Sam eyed the gunman casually and tried to put a name to his face. He had seen the reward posters on Hobden and his men that Tate was carrying, and he finally decided that this man must be Vance Felton.

'I did see a sheriff and some men heading back along the trail some hours ago, but they were pretty badly shot up and in no mood to stop and talk to me,' he answered, and as he spoke he slowly lowered his hands down to rest on the saddle pommel in front of him.

A deep laugh escaped Felton, and he lowered the muzzle of his rifle towards the ground as he began to relax in the youngster's company. 'Were any of these men with the sheriff dead?' he asked.

'At least ten,' Sam exaggerated, but it got the desired effect when the gunman burst out laughing once again. The young bounty-hunter quickly seized the opportunity offered and grabbed for his six-gun. His draw was quick and fluid, and the outlaw's face registered shock when he focused on the weapon in the youngster's hand.

'You'd better put that thing away before you get yourself badly hurt, youngster,' he warned ominously.

'You're the one who will get hurt if you don't put that rifle down on the ground,' Sam replied evenly. 'And just remember that this isn't some sixteen-year-old girl you're dealing with this time.'

'What's that supposed to mean?' Felton asked.

'It means that I found that young girl who suffered at your hands last night on the trail leading into Mitchell Wells. It also means that I'm looking for any reason to kill you for what you did to her, so please go ahead and do me a favour by trying something.'

'I didn't touch her,' Felton declared anxiously. 'Tyler Hobden raped her, and shot her father as well.'

'You sat around and let him do it,' Sam accused angrily. 'That makes you as guilty as he is.'

Felton's reply to this was to swing the muzzle of his rifle up and to snap off a quick shot at Sam. The hastily aimed bullet plucked at the young bounty-hunter's shirt-sleeve, but this didn't seem to register in his mind as he returned the outlaw's fire. His shot was deliberate and accurate, and the single bullet caught the gunman in the right shoulder and spun him around to fall backwards to the ground.

Sam slid down off his horse and walked across to where his victim lay moaning on the ground. He threw Felton's rifle aside and then did the same with the six-gun that he removed from his holster. He then knelt down beside the outlaw and placed the muzzle of his six-gun against his temple.

'I want some questions answered, Felton,' he declared evenly. 'And if you don't answer them I'll leave you out here to die.'

The outlaw was seriously wounded, and his breathing was laboured from the pain caused by his smashed shoulder. He looked up at Sam and his eyes clearly showed the pain that he was feeling from the wound.

Sam didn't bother to wait for him to

speak, but instead asked his first question. 'Where's Hobden?'

Felton knew that his only hope of surviving his injury was to get into a town where there was a doctor who could mend his smashed shoulder. He also knew that he'd need this youngster to help him reach that town, so he decided that if all he was after was information about Hobden, he could have it.

'He went on ahead with Ray and Wilby, and I was supposed to catch up with them later,' he replied through clenched teeth to suppress the pain.

'Where are they heading?'

The outlaw waited until the pain had eased some before answering. 'They're heading for a cabin located in the mountains to the north-west of here. Wilby Dixan's father and brother live up there.'

Sam recalled what Tate had said about one of Hobden's men being from around these parts, and now it all tied in. The young bounty-hunter abruptly climbed to his feet and reholstered his six-gun before turning to walk back to his horse. His desire to catch up with the outlaw leader was overpowering, and he wanted to get moving before Tate and the others could arrive and hold him back.

'What about me?' Felton demanded from behind him.

'You're just lucky that I didn't kill you outright, and that I want Hobden more than you,' the youngster growled back over his shoulder at the outlaw without slackening his pace.

The crack of a handgun being discharged from behind Sam caused him to throw himself sideways to the ground, but not before he felt the searing pain of the bullet as it grazed his upper right arm. Hitting the ground, he rolled over to come back up onto his knees facing the wounded outlaw, and his six-gun was ready in his hand. On seeing Felton taking aim for a second shot with the small-calibre pistol that he was holding in his left hand, Sam quickly fired off two shots and hit the outlaw in the chest with both. Felton then slumped backwards onto the ground and showed no further signs of movement.

'Damn it,' Sam muttered to himself as he climbed to his feet and warily moved back over to where the outlaw lay. Both of his bullets had found their mark, and blood was now soaking the front of Vance Felton's shirt.

The young bounty-hunter wrenched the pistol from the outlaw's hand and threw it aside before checking him for signs of life, but found none. Sam then sat back on his haunches and considered how lucky he had been. Felton had been carrying a hide-away gun, and would have surely shot him in the middle of the back if he'd had full use of his right hand, but instead he had been forced to use his left hand and this had acted to save the youngster's life.

Just then the sound of horses approaching him along the trail from the south could be heard, and Sam looked up to see Tate and the others closing in on him at speed.

EIGHT

The sun was slowly easing towards the western horizon, and the shadows were now lengthening significantly. Sam looked across at Tate to see if he was showing any signs of easing off in readiness to make camp for the night, but the old bounty-hunter's eyes were fixed solidly on the trail in front of him.

Tate Sharp was a very angry man, and he

hadn't spoken to Sam since leaving the place where he had killed Felton some two hours before. The old bounty-hunter had given his younger companion a thorough dressing-down over the fact that he'd nearly got himself killed by not waiting for them – a point that was clearly underpinned by the fact that Sam was now carrying a deep bullet-graze on his upper right arm. The reprimanding that the youngster had endured in front of Bob Ward and Duke Baxter had served to embarrass him deeply, but he'd accepted it without protest because he realized just how close he had come to death at the outlaw's hands by going it alone.

Vance Felton's body had been bundled in a ground-sheet and tied across his horse, and that now was being led along on a long rein by Sam. The dead outlaw had a big reward on his head, and Tate intended taking his body to the nearest law office to claim the reward.

Finally the old bounty-hunter held up his right hand and called a halt. 'The tracks are getting too hard to see and we stand a good chance of losing them if we continue on in this light,' he announced. 'So I suggest we make camp now and then continue on in the morning.'

His three companions readily agreed and they all moved off the trail to set up camp for the night under a stand of trees. They hobbled their horses in amongst the trees where there was plenty of grass for them to eat, and Vance Felton's body was left tied across the saddle of his horse to save them the trouble of having to load it again in the morning.

A meal of beans and biscuits was prepared by the trail-weary men, and when they were finally settling down for the night Sam decided to attempt to make peace with his old friend once again. 'I am sorry about what happened today, Tate,' he apologized. 'And I know that I was just plain stupid in what I did.'

The old bounty-hunter shook his head wearily and it took him a moment before he replied. 'You gave me one hell of a fright today, Sam, and if you ever do anything like that again I will shoot you myself.'

A slow smile eased Sam's features as he considered what his companion had just said. It was Tate's way of saying that he believed Sam had very nearly committed the sin of thinking only of himself and forgetting his partner. The one rule that the old bounty-hunter had always taught Sam was that a partner is someone to be relied on, someone to protect your back, and someone to read the last rites over your grave – and that to allow your personal troubles to become more important than your partner was practically the same as shooting your friend in the back.

'How is that shoulder of yours?' Tate asked as a smile also settled on his lips.

'It's stiffening up a mite now that the night air is getting into it,' his young companion replied.

'Sleep close to the fire tonight to keep it warm, and then first thing in the morning go and exercise it to take the stiffness out of the muscle,' the old bounty-hunter advised him.

The four men then settled down for the night and were soon asleep. They were all dog-tired from their long day in the saddle, but their natural instinct made them sleep lightly and awaken at the slightest sound that was out of the normal.

The night passed without incident, and it was the sound of the pans being set on the fire stones in readiness to cook breakfast that woke Sam. He rolled over to see that the other three men were already up and busily packing up their gear in preparation for the day ahead. The sun was still low in the cast and Sam guessed that it was around 6 a.m. He suddenly remembered the watch that he had in his breast pocket and he pulled it out to examine it. On opening its front cover he found that it read 6.12 a.m., and he allowed his mind to settle back onto the frail young girl who had given it to him the day before. His heart still heaved when he thought of her, but the burning anger that he had felt was now a grim determination that he would stick to Hobden's trail until the outlaw had paid for the hurt he had inflicted on Sarah and her father.

'You'd better get up and exercise that injured shoulder of yours,' Tate advised his young companion from where he was kneeling down beside the camp-fire.

Sam knew that the old bounty-hunter still felt uncertain about his emotional stability, and he thought he should try to put him at ease. 'I guess I went off my head a bit yesterday, but I promise you that I've settled down now.'

'Never forget the anger that you felt yesterday, and how your emotions can sometimes be your worst enemy,' the old bounty-hunter advised him. 'Now you go off and exercise that shoulder, and I'll have some breakfast ready for you when you come back.'

The young bounty-hunter pulled his boots on and rolled up his bed-roll. He then bid good-morning to his other two travelling-companions before leaving the campsite to find somewhere private to work the stiffness out of his shoulder. He found an open area in amongst the rocks and began a set routine of arm and upper body movements that Tate had taught him to loosen his shoulder muscles, and to make them smooth and fluid in operation. He had finished the routine and was attempting a couple of practice quick draws when he sensed that someone was approaching him from behind. In one fluid movement he spun around and levelled his six-gun on the intruder.

Duke Baxter quickly raised both his hands in the air to indicate that he offered no danger to the youngster, and smiled when he saw an angry frown settle on Sam's brow.

'That was some deadly move you made there,' he declared, but on getting no response from the youngster he decided to explain his presence. 'Tate asked me to come and tell you that breakfast will be ready in ten minutes.'

'I'll be there,' Sam assured him as he reholstered his six-gun and waited for the deputy sheriff to leave.

Baxter instead sat down on a nearby rock and eyed the young bounty-hunter with interest. 'You've got yourself a good quickdraw there, Sam,' he declared. 'But you move your head around too much when you're drawing the weapon.'

'Is that so,' Sam replied coolly, but then remembered that Tate had said the deputy was the quickest draw he would ever see, and curiosity got the better of him as he thought about the observation. 'Will that slow down my quickdraw any?'

'Yes, and it will make it harder to hit your target when you fire,' Baxter advised him as he climbed to his feet and faced up to Sam. 'You make ready to draw on me, but please don't shoot.'

Sam did as he was bid and locked eyes with the deputy as he waited calmly for the first sign of movement towards his weapon. They stood facing each other for a full ten seconds before Baxter finally made his move – but the move wasn't what Sam expected. It was the deputy's boot in the dirt that made a scraping sound loud enough to momentarily draw Sam's attention, and when the youngster looked up again he was shocked to find that the deputy already had his six-gun levelled on him.

'You're dead, Sam,' Baxter informed him calmly. 'If you ever hope to survive in a face-to-face gunfight with the best you must learn to shut out everything around you and watch your opponent's eyes. That's where you will see the first sign that they are about to draw their weapon, and if you move your eyes off them you are as good as dead.'

Sam took a deep breath to steady his tingling nerves. He had been tricked, but to make it worse he had fallen for it hook, line and sinker. He now realized that Duke Baxter was every bit as good as Tate had claimed, and he also realized that this was an opportunity where he could get coaching from a professional gunfighter.

'Tate has always told me to keep my wits about me just in case there is someone else thinking about buying into the fight,' he explained confusedly. 'How can you do the two things at once?'

Baxter sat back down on the rock and waited until Sam had sat down beside him before he spoke. 'Tate is right. You must always know what is happening around you before, during, and after the gunfight. First you must learn to reduce the odds against you by making sure that the fight is set up on your terms. Make your opponent come to you, and try to make them feel that the terrain is against them from the start. Try to decide if there are any bystanders who could be involved with your opponent, and if you will need to cover that possibility after the gunfight. Make good use of your side vision to check for movement that could indicate that there are other people involved, and always check the area after the fight to make sure that it's all clear – but when you are in the middle of the gunfight focus only on your opponent and don't move your head or eyes, or you will end up dead.'

Sam thought about what he had just heard and realized that it was very good advice, but he had one question in his mind that still needed answering. 'Can we try that draw one more time?' he asked innocently.

'I'd like to know as well,' the deputy smiled as if reading the youngster's mind. 'I guess we're all the same, it doesn't matter how old we are.'

Sam climbed back to his feet and moved back out into the open to face Baxter once again. He locked eyes with the deputy, and tried to ease the tension in his arms as he waited for the first sign of intent from his opponent. Baxter once again moved his boot in the dirt, but this time the youngster took it as a signal to draw the weapon. His hand was a blur of movement as he lifted his six-gun from its holster, but his mind registered surprise when he saw that the deputy was even faster and that his six-gun was levelled a split second earlier than his own.

The two men stood facing each other for several seconds with their weapons levelled without moving. The adrenalin was pumping through their veins as if it was a real life situation, and it was the deputy who lowered his weapon first and gave out a slow whistle.

'With a bit of practice you'll be one of the best,' he declared as he reholstered his six-gun.

Sam slid his own weapon back into its holster, and then took a deep breath to steady his jangled nerves. He knew that if it had been a real gunfight there was every chance he would now be dead, and his only hope of survival would have lain in the faint chance that his aim was better than Baxter's on the day. He was still standing pondering this thought when he heard Tate's voice call out his name.

'What the hell are you up to?' the old bounty-hunter asked as he walked into the clearing and saw them standing facing each other.

'It's okay, Tate,' the deputy sheriff assured him. 'I was just giving the youngster a few tips on how to improve his quickdraw.'

'He's every bit as fast as you said, Tate,' Sam declared as he turned to face his old companion.

'So now you know just how expensive that drink would've been back in Mitchell Wells?' Tate asked, and smiled on seeing the discomfort this caused his young companion.

'Let's go back and get some breakfast before Bob eats it all,' Duke Baxter suggested, and all three headed off back towards the campsite.

NINE

Tyler Hobden jerked awake. Something had awoken him, and he lay quietly on the old wooden bunk as he listened to the noises around him. It was late afternoon and the heat of the day was cooling noticeably as the sun slowly sank towards the western mountain range.

The sound of muted conversation coming from the main room of the cabin finally drew Hobden's interest, and he silently climbed to his feet and crossed to the doorway. He couldn't quite make out what was being said by the men on the other side of the door, so he palmed his six-gun and pulled the door wide open. Four men were seated around an old wooden table that was positioned in the middle of the room, and they looked around in surprise as he entered.

'What's going on in here?' the outlaw leader demanded.

The four men looked at each other nervously, and none seemed too keen to answer the question. Ray Vidler sat at the far end of the table flanked by his father, Lucas, and his brother, Mike – and Wilby Dixan sat at the near end of the table with his back to Hobden, but it was Ray Vidler who finally spoke out.

'We were thinking that we might share out the money from the Mitchell Wells bank job soon,' he stated.

'You were thinking!' Hobden scoffed. 'And I suppose you were also thinking that we are safe enough up here that we don't need to keep a lookout?'

This comment caused Ray Vidler to squirm in his seat as he realized that it was he who was supposed to be outside watching the trail to the cabin. 'I thought I'd come in and talk to you and Wilby about splitting up the money, and I've only been in here for a short time,' he quickly assured the outlaw leader.

'You seem to be making a lot of decisions lately, Ray,' Hobden growled. 'Maybe you've decided that it's time you took over the running of this outfit as well?'

'No, but I have decided I'm not going with you when you leave here,' Vidler announced defiantly. 'I'm going to settle down here and enjoy this money for a while.'

'I see,' Hobden stated coolly. 'And I suppose it was your idea that we split the money up now too?'

Ray Vidler noted the ominous tone of Hobden's voice and watched warily as he reholstered his six-gun. He had seen this same situation develop some months back when another member of the gang had made the mistake of questioning one of Hobden's decisions, and that had ended up with him paying for it with his life.

'I'm not pushing for any trouble, Tyler,' he assured him quickly. 'I just want to stay behind when you leave.'

'It seems to me that you're running out on us,' Hobden challenged, but before Vidler could answer this Hobden's name was called out loudly by someone outside the cabin.

'Come out with your hands in the air,' the voice went on to demand. 'We've got your cabin surrounded.'

The outlaws quickly rushed to the windows with their weapons drawn, but there was no-one to be seen in the yard area at the front of the cabin – leaving the heavy brush growing outside the yard area as the likely hiding-place for the person who had shouted out the challenge.

'Go into the bedroom and cover the back, Wilby,' Hobden instructed, and waited until he had disappeared through the bedroom doorway before turning his attention back to the others. 'It's most likely that posse from Mitchell Wells. If it is, we'll have to wait until after dark and then make a break for it.'

'You must've done a great job of covering your tracks if they found you this easily,' Lucas Vidler snarled angrily, but failed to see the look of irritation that this comment brought from Hobden.

'Who the hell's out there?' the outlaw leader demanded loudly in a voice that showed this displeasure.

'You'll find that out when you give yourself up,' the voice replied.

Ray Vidler snapped off several quick shots from his six-gun in the direction that he thought the voice had come from, but this only served to annoy Hobden even further.

'Hold your fire, you damned fool,' he growled. 'You'll never hit anything with that six-shooter at this range. Go get your rifle, and then save your ammunition until you're sure you've got a target to shoot at.'

Tate Sharp lay in the cover of a fallen log and watched the cabin closely. All of Ray Vidler's shots had so far been well wide of him, but he kept low to the ground and very still so as not to give away his hiding-place to the outlaws inside the cabin. It had turned out to be a remarkably successful day for him and his companions in their search for the outlaws' cabin. They'd lost the outlaws' tracks on entering the rocky foot-hills of the mountains, and even with Tate's years of experience at tracking they were unable to locate them again. After finally giving up the search for the tracks in the rough terrain, they had agreed to head further up into the mountains in hope of finding some sign of the outlaws' tracks once again. It was getting close to two o'clock in the afternoon when they had made their lucky break and came across a miner's cabin built at the side of a mountain stream.

The grizzle-headed old man who had met them with a shotgun in his hands was pleased to be able to give them the exact location of the Vidlers' cabin. He'd informed them that for many years he had been the victim of the Vidler family's stand over tactics, and that he had been forced to pay them for the right to live on their mountain from small amounts of gold that he found in nearby creeks.

It had been an easy task to follow the old prospector's directions, and their luck had continued when they found that Hobden hadn't bothered to maintain a lookout on the trail leading to the cabin. The four men had quickly moved in on the cabin on foot, and whilst Tate and Sam took up position at the front of the cabin, Bob Ward and Duke Baxter had moved around to cover the rear.

'Are you coming out, Hobden, or do we

have to burn you out?' the old bounty-hunter shouted from his cover.

This brought about another burst of gunfire from the men inside the cabin, only this time it was from rifles and it came much closer to Tate's position. He looked across at his young companion, who was lying in cover some thirty feet away to his right. The youngster had his rifle in his hands, and on receiving a signal from his old friend he took aim on one of the cabin windows. Tate then put his hat on the end of a long stick and raised it in the air and waved it about amongst the bushes. The response from the outlaws inside the cabin was instantaneous, and a volley of rifle-shots rang out – with several of the bullets striking both the hat and stick.

Sam's rifle cracked once as he fired in return, and the rifle-fire from the cabin instantly eased and then finally stopped as a voice called out inside the cabin.

Lucas Vidler lay dead on the cabin floor. There was blood staining the front of his shirt, and his face looked as if he was asleep. No-one had spoken since Mike Vidler had shouted out to his brother that their father had been hit, and now both brothers were kneeling beside their father with disbelief written on their faces. Ray Vidler finally looked up at Tyler Hobden with hatred plainly written on his face.

'This is your fault, Hobden,' he accused. 'And if we get out of here alive I'm going to make you pay for it.'

Hobden replied to this by smiling amiably. 'You won't have to worry about getting out of here alive if you don't get back to that window and keep your eyes open.'

'Come on, Mike, you cover that end window and I'll cover this one,' Ray Vidler encouraged his brother reluctantly.

'I'll go and check on Wilby, and don't go firing those rifles until you are sure you can hit something,' Hobden announced before crossing the room and entering the bedroom where he found Wilby Dixan keeping watch out through the rear window.

'Is there anyone out the back?' the outlaw leader asked his companion.

'Ain't seen anyone yet,' Dixan replied easily. 'What was that ruckus out the front all about?'

Hobden crossed to the window and had a quick look outside before finally answering. 'Old Lucas caught a bullet in the chest, and is dead.'

'Do you think that's the posse out there?' Dixan asked.

Hobden was about to answer this when a voice called out his name from the scrub at the rear of the cabin. 'Hobden, this is Deputy Sheriff Duke Baxter. And I'm warning you to give yourself up before we're forced to burn you out.'

The outlaw leader fired off several quick shots in reply to this voice, and then crossed the room to lie back on the bed.

'You got a plan to get us out of here? Dixan asked.

The outlaw leader laughed drily before answering. 'You know that I've always got a plan, Wilby. You just wake me when it's dark outside, and I'll get us out of this hole real easy like.'

The short burst of rifle-fire from the rear window of the cabin had caused Duke Baxter to hug the ground beside Bob Ward. 'I think it's going to take some time before we convince these hombres to give themselves up to us,' he concluded drily.

Bob Ward merely nodded his head in reply, and listened with interest to the renewed burst of rifle-fire from the front of the cabin. He was a man of very few words, and had already realized that it was going to be a long wait before the men inside the cabin would surrender. But his abhorrence at what Hobden and his men had done to Sarah Sainsbury and her father was his motivation for being here, and he was quite prepared to wait.

The sun was now well out of sight behind the distant mountains and it was getting darker by the minute. Tate Sharp raised his head and took aim on one of the windows at the front of the cabin. Most of the rifle-fire had come from the men inside the cabin, and only occasionally had he or Sam returned their fire. A flitting shadow showed at the corner of the cabin's window, so the old bounty-hunter quickly aimed his rifle and squeezed the trigger. The rifle kicked back against the shoulder, but he knew instantly that his bullet had failed to find its intended target.

Sam waved his hand to catch Tate's attention, and then signalled the old bounty-hunter to give him some covering fire while he moved in closer to the cabin. He then pulled his legs up under himself and waited for the covering fire to begin.

Tate took careful aim at the left-hand

window of the cabin and fired his rifle, and then alternated his fire at the front windows in quick time.

Sam was already on the move as the second shot sounded out and was running across the open ground with his rifle clutched in his hand. He made the cover of a woodpile located some yards from the front of the cabin without a shot being fired at him, and he lay there without moving for several moments to catch his breath.

Duke Baxter had listened to this rifle-fire from his position at the rear of the cabin. 'It sounds like Tate is laying down some covering fire out there,' he stated.

Bob Ward nodded his head in agreement. 'Maybe I should go around to help them?' he offered.

Duke Baxter voiced his agreement to this suggestion and watched as the farmer moved off through the brush towards the front of the cabin. He then turned his full attention back to the single window at the back of the cabin, and watched it intently through the gloomy darkness.

Wilby Dixan turned from the window and spoke. 'Are you awake, Tyler?' he asked.

'Yes, Wilby,' Hobden replied as he sat up and stretched luxuriously. 'Have you seen anyone out there yet?'

'I think I saw one hombre moving off to the left a few minutes ago,' he replied. 'He's probably gone around the front to help the others firing on Ray and Mike.'

'I'd better go in and check to see that they are still holding them back,' Hobden informed his companion. 'While I'm gone see if you can kick those boards off the end wall over there in the corner.'

The outlaw leader then walked through to the other room where he found both Ray and Mike Vidler hunkered down out of harm's way by their windows, neither of them seeming too keen on exposing themselves to gunfire from outside.

'You bloody fools,' Hobden growled as he moved across to the window and looked outside. He instantly spotted the shape of Sam lying behind the woodpile, and nearly paid for it with his life when a bullet splintered the window-frame just inches from his face.

'One of them has managed to move up behind that pile of wood out there, all because you two are too yellow to show your damn faces,' he spat out angrily. 'If you want to get out of this place alive I suggest you get that posse man out there before he gets you.'

'We don't have to do what you say any more, Hobden,' Ray Vidler replied indignantly. 'It's all your fault that the posse is out there in the first place.'

'That isn't the large posse from Mitchell Wells out there,' he explained calmly. 'By the sound of their rifle-fire it's a much smaller posse of around four men. So if you want to end up like your father there, just stay here and do nothing – or do as I say and live.'

The two brothers looked at each other and they seemed to reach agreement without speaking, and it was Ray Vidler who voiced their decision. 'Okay, we'll do as you say for the moment, but we're taking our share of the money and going our own way once we're clear of this place.'

'I don't give a damn what you two do once we're out of here,' Hobden proclaimed easily. 'Now, this is what I've planned. Wilby is out the back knocking the boards off the end wall so we can get out that way. But we have to keep them busy out the front until we're ready to make a run for it. So get back to your windows and keep firing until we're ready to leave.'

'You stay in here with us,' Mike Vidler demanded as the outlaw leader made to turn and head back into the bedroom. 'I don't trust you one little bit, Hobden.'

'I've got to go out to help Wilby to prepare the escape route,' Hobden declared angrily. 'If you're that worried about me I'll leave the saddle-bags containing the money in here with you until we're ready to move out.'

Ray Vidler readily accepted this idea. 'Okay, but make sure you put them over here beside me so I can keep an eye on them.'

Hobden carried the saddle-bags across and placed them on the floor beside Ray Vidler, and was further incensed when Vidler opened one of the bags to check its contents.

'Not that I don't trust you, Tyler,' he declared. 'But to tell the truth, I don't.'

The outlaw leader bit back his anger and walked from the room without speaking. The two brothers then moved back to their windows and started firing out into the night. They kept up a steady pattern of fire, and it only eased when they stopped to reload. The return fire from the men outside was spasmodic, and the brothers began to feel much more confident as the minutes passed by. Finally Hobden returned to the room and moved across to stand next to Ray Vidler at the window.

'We're ready to go now. You two lay down some covering fire before bolting out through the hole we've made in the bedroom wall,' he instructed as he picked up the saddle-bags and made to head back towards the bedroom door. 'Me and Wilby will be waiting for you with the horses.'

'Hold it!' Ray Vidler demanded as he swung his rifle around to cover the outlaw leader. 'The money goes with us just in case you decide to leave without us.'

Mike Vidler also swung his rifle onto Hobden to show that the decision was unanimous, but he made the fatal mistake of exposing himself at the window. A rifle-bullet caught him squarely in the side of the head, and he was dead before he hit the floor where he lay in the widening pool of his own blood.

The shock caused by his brother's sudden death stunned Ray Vidler, and he stood looking at his brother's body with disbelief written on his face. This disbelief turned to rage, and he turned back to the window and began firing wildly at the men outside the cabin.

Tyler Hobden slid his six-gun from his holster and fired a single shot at Vidler's head – killing him instantly. The outlaw leader then gave out an insane laugh before swinging the full saddle-bags up onto his shoulder and walking from the room.

Tate Sharp heard the single handgun-shot and noted that there was no longer any rifle-fire coming from inside the cabin. He wondered at its meaning, but his attention was drawn to Bob Ward as he moved in beside him.

'I've come around to give you two a hand,' the farmer announced. 'But it sounds like it's quietened down now.'

'Most of their shooting has been pretty wide so far,' the old bounty-hunter assured him. 'So we've had an easy time of it really. Sam has even moved up closer behind that woodpile so he can get a better shot at them.'

Sam had also noted the lack of rifle-fire since hearing the single shot fired from the handgun, and was trying to decide whether he should move in closer on the cabin when he heard the pounding of horse-hooves at the back of the building. The young bounty-hunter jumped to his feet and ran towards the end of the cabin, arriving just in time to see two horsemen disappearing into the night. He snapped off several shots at their retreating backs, but the outlaws were quickly swallowed up by the darkness.

'Damn it!' he spat out angrily in disappointment. He realized that he could do nothing now to stop the escaping outlaws, so he instead made his way back along to the front door of the cabin and pushed it wide open. Through the doorway he could see the shapes of several dark figures huddled on the floor, and realized that they weren't showing any signs of movement. He entered the cabin and nudged one figure with his toe, but the figure remained limp and lifeless.

The young bounty-hunter moved across to the table where an oil-lamp stood and put a match to its wick. The lamp flickered into life, and then slowly illuminated the whole room as it began to burn steadily. Sam could now easily see the three men lying on the floor, but he didn't bother about them as he moved across to the bedroom door. He eased the door wide open, and let the light from the lamp illuminate the bedroom.

'Damn,' he muttered as he realized that this room was completely empty. He then turned and crossed to the front door, where he shouted out to his companions. 'It's all clear in here,' he announced before turning his attention back to the dead men lying on the floor. He rolled each body over and checked their faces, and was just finishing when Tate and Bob entered the cabin.

'Tyler Hobden got away,' the youngster stated before the other two men could speak.

'They must've shot Duke Baxter to be able to get away that easily,' Bob Ward declared uneasily before turning back towards the front door. 'I'll go out and check to see what's happened to him.'

Tate Sharp took the lamp out of the youngster's hand and examined the faces of the three dead men. 'It looks as if we've managed to wipe out the Vidler family in one easy effort,' he announced. 'It's a shame we didn't manage to get Hobden as well though.'

Further discussion was quickly put aside as Bob Ward re-entered the cabin carrying a semi-conscious Duke Baxter over his shoulder. 'I found him lying out back amongst the bushes,' the giant of a farmer informed them as he lowered the deputy onto a chair.

'See if you can find some water, Sam,' Tate instructed his young companion.

Sam did as he was bid and moved off across the room to a cupboard built into the wall, and returned with a bucket full of fresh water and a tin mug. He placed them on the floor beside the old bounty-hunter, who soaked his neckerchief in the water and then set about moistening the deputy sheriff's face and neck. Once Baxter started to regain his senses, Tate filled the tin mug with water and held it to Duke's lips so he could drink.

The deputy recovered quickly, but his voice was still thick as he spoke. 'What the hell hit me?' he asked.

'We were hoping that you could tell us?' Tate queried as he refilled the mug and passed it back to the deputy.

'I was watching the back window of the cabin from the cover of the bushes when I heard a noise behind me, and as I went to look around someone hit me,' he explained, and groaned loudly when he put his fingers to the tender area at the side of his head.

'The end wall has been kicked out of the cabin, so it was probably Hobden or one of his men who managed to get around behind you,' Sam declared. 'And I'd say you are lucky that they didn't shoot you – but then I guess they didn't want to make any noise that would highlight the fact that they were making a break for it.'

'The way my head feels at the moment I'm not too sure I should thank them for that,' the deputy groaned.

'Well, I think you'll live anyway,' Tate announced as he examined the bruising on the side of the deputy's head. 'But I suggest that we stay here for the night to give you the chance to rest up, and we should be able to pick up Hobden's tracks easily enough in the morning.'

The others agreed with his suggestion, and Sam and Bob then left the cabin to bring the horses in from where they had left them back down the trail.

TEN

Tyler Hobden and Wilby Dixan reined in their horses and sat looking back in the direction from which they had just ridden. It was now mid-evening and the moon was lighting up the landscape around them like daylight. This allowed them to stop and check to see if there was any sign of the posse from the Vidlers' cabin on the trail behind them.

'Can you see anything?' Dixan asked.

'Be quiet,' Hobden growled at his companion. 'How the hell can I hear anything with you yabbering away?'

Dixan took this rebuff from the outlaw leader without comment. He realized that Ray Vidler and his brother were both now dead, and that he would be wise to stay on the right side of Tyler Hobden – even if it meant pandering to his ego for a while.

'It looks okay so far,' Hobden commented as he turned to face his companion. 'But at least we now know what we're up against, and we've got time to get into Logan and set up a welcoming committee for them.'

Dixan merely nodded his head in agreement with this, but knew little of what the outlaw leader was talking about or what he was planning to do when he reached Logan.

In the distance the lights of Logan could be seen, and Hobden surveyed them for a moment before speaking. 'When we reach town we'll head straight for the saloon to see if there's anyone around that we know,' he advised his companion. 'We'll have to find some men and organize an ambush pretty damn quick if we hope to be ready for those possemen.'

'You can depend on me, Tyler!' Dixan replied quickly.

The outlaw leader didn't bother to reply to this, but instead pushed his horse into a canter towards the distant town. He knew that Wilby Dixan was afraid of him, and it made him feel good. It had always brought pleasure to him to know that his men were afraid of him, and at times he would deliberately harass them just to see that fear come into their eyes, but at the moment he was delighted with himself that he'd managed to reduce the number of people who would've expected a share of the money taken from the Mitchell Wells bank. He knew that it was going to cost him a lot of money to hire the men to set up an ambush for the posse, but if his plan came off and he managed to kill Wilby Dixan in the process, it would mean that all the remaining money would then be his.

The street was dark and gloomy as the two outlaws rode towards the town centre. The moon wasn't high enough in the sky yet to light up the street, and the shadows thrown by the buildings that lined the street were causing this gloomy effect. The two outlaws drew their horses to a halt outside the front of the double-storey saloon. They dismounted and tied off their mounts to the hitching-rail before climbing the steps and entering the saloon through the batwing doors. Both men stopped just inside the doorway and eyed the human contents of the bar-room. There were fourteen men inside the room, and a single woman sitting at a table playing cards with three of these men. There was a white-haired old barman standing behind the bar at the far end of the room talking to a couple of cowboys, and the rest of the men were scattered around the room at the tables.

Hobden ran an eye over the men in the room but failed to recognize any of them. He was disappointed that there was no-one in the bar-room that he knew, but this didn't show on his face as he allowed his gaze to settle back onto the woman playing cards. She was in her mid-forties, and even at that age she was still a very handsome woman. She was dressed in a long, flowing, maroon-coloured velvet dress that had a deep-cut neckline that easily showed off her ample bosom, and as the outlaw leader watched her she raised her eyes and looked directly at him. Her eyes were of a jade-green colour, and Hobden found his pulse quicken as his gaze met hers.

'Let's get out of here,' the outlaw leader growled to Dixan as he forced himself to bring his mind back to the task at hand. He then did an abrupt about-face and pushed through the batwing doors into the street.

'We've got to find the sheriff's office,' he announced, to the surprise of his companion.

'The sheriff's office?' Dixan queried, thinking this would've been the last place on earth that Hobden would be seeking when he had a posse so close on his heels.

'Yeah, the sheriff's office,' Hobden growled irritably. 'You got a problem with that?'

'No – not at all,' Dixan replied hastily, and followed after the outlaw leader as they walked along the street towards the law office.

The sheriff's office was a single-storey building built mainly of mud-brick and timber. The walls were thick and sturdy, and the glass-panelled windows at the front of the building were encased in iron bars. There were no lights to be seen from inside the building when the two outlaws stopped outside to look it over, but this didn't seem to deter Hobden when he walked up and hammered noisily on the front door.

'Open up, you lazy good-for-nothing,' he shouted, and a chuckle escaped him when he saw a light suddenly appear through the windows. 'Come on, Morgan, we haven't got all night.'

The heavy wooden door rattled noisily in its frame as someone unlocked it from the inside, and it swung open to reveal a middle-aged man wearing nothing but his underwear and a gunbelt strapped around his waist.

'Who is it?' he asked as he tried to focus his sleep-laden eyes on the men at the door, but on recognizing the outlaw leader's face he seemed to physically sag.

'It's good to see you again, Morgan,' the outlaw leader proclaimed as he pushed past him into the law office and then stood surveying the room.

The sheriff was now sweating profusely as he watched the outlaw leader with eyes that clearly showed the fear he held for the man. He wiped the sweat from his eyes with his sleeve before finally replying. 'Tyler, what are you doing here in Logan?'

Hobden ignored this question and moved across to sit down in the swivel-chair behind the desk. 'Wilby Dixan, meet Sheriff Morgan Stratford – an old friend of mine.'

Wilby Dixan had already entered the office and was now standing watching the two men, and he nodded his head in greeting at the lawman without speaking.

'Are you just passing through, Tyler?' the sheriff asked as he moved across to stand near the desk. He was hoping with all his heart that the answer would be yes, and that he would soon be back living the quiet life that he'd been enjoying these past two years.

'I need your help, Morgan,' Hobden informed him.

'What can I possibly do to help you, Tyler?' the sheriff asked nervously.

'I've got a posse close on my heels, and I need some men to help ambush them. I've already been over to the saloon to see if there was anyone I knew, but there were only townsfolk there. I'll need at least six men who are good with rifles.'

The sheriff paused while he thought over this request. He had managed to set up a lucrative side-business in the town by offering safe haven to small-time outlaws for a price. These men lived in a group of shacks located to the north of the town and they usually kept pretty well to themselves, but Morgan knew that they would do anything for money.

'I think that I might be able to help you,' he declared with a new energy in his voice. He then went on to tell Hobden about these men and the kind of money they would be asking to carry out his task.

'Okay, go and get them now,' the outlaw leader directed. 'And tell them I'll pay a bonus of five hundred dollars for every member of the posse that they kill.'

The sheriff quickly dressed and then went off into the night to find the men. He soon returned to his office with the nine gunmen in tow, and waited nervously while Hobden ran a critical eye over them.

'Beggars can't be choosers,' the outlaw leader finally commented before going on to outline his plan to the men.

'The posse could be here any time between now and tomorrow morning. We'll take up position at the saloon, and wait there for them to arrive.'

'The saloon?' the sheriff quizzed. 'Wouldn't you be better off waiting for them out on the trail somewhere?'

'No – we're going to wait right here in town,' Hobden replied. 'If there is a problem with that you'd better tell me about it now.'

'There's no problem at all,' the sheriff quickly assured him. 'I was just thinking that maybe it would be easier to ambush them out in the open – that's all.'

'You leave the thinking to me in future, and you'll live much longer, Morgan,' Hobden warned before returning his attention back to his plan. 'We will move on over to the saloon as soon as I've finished here and get ready for the posse. I want one man to position himself on the upper floor of the building across the street from the saloon, and five more at the upstairs windows of the saloon, and the last three downstairs with me and Wilby. If the posse doesn't show before dawn, I'll need one man to ride out and keep watch on the trail to the south – and it'll be his job to ride in and warn us when they are coming. Are there any questions about what I just told you?'

One man cleared his throat and spoke out on behalf of the other eight gunmen. 'Sheriff Stratford told us that we would receive two hundred dollars each to help you – so can we have the money now?'

Tyler Hobden eyed the man over with interest. 'What's your name?' he asked.

'Tod Gordon,' the outlaw replied.

'To answer your question, Gordon – no,' Hobden informed him coolly. 'I will pay you your money when the posse has been destroyed, and a bonus of five hundred dollars for every posseman you kill. Are there any more questions?'

The local outlaws looked at each other but none of them spoke out. They would have liked to have the money paid up front, but they didn't want to jeopardize the offer by pushing the issue with Hobden.

'Let's move across to the saloon now,' Hobden directed them. 'Just go in as if you are going to have a drink, and then wait until me and Wilby have secured the place before you get involved.'

'I should stay here,' the sheriff declared quickly. 'The local townsfolk will expect me to do something if they see me in there with you.'

'That's a good idea, Morgan,' Hobden conceded, realizing that the sheriff was of better value to him as the local trusted lawman, than as a member of his gang. 'I'll see you later if I need you.'

The sheriff watched the men file out of the door behind the outlaw leader, and wondered what the near future held for him. He had to somehow keep out of sight until this was all over, and then reappear as if he knew nothing about it. He sat back down behind his desk and allowed his mind to work on this problem.

Kate Brown looked up from the table where she was playing cards and watched the men as they filed into the bar-room. It was close to midnight and the saloon-owner wondered why these men had suddenly decided to frequent her saloon. They moved across to the bar and ordered drinks from the barman, and then stood around in a group sipping at their drinks and talking amongst themselves. It all seemed peaceful enough to Kate, but she couldn't help but feel uneasy about their presence in her saloon.

'Come on, Kate. What are you betting?' one of the men sitting at her table prompted her. She looked back at the cards in her hand, but found it impossible to concentrate on the game. 'I fold,' she announced, before placing her cards face down on the table. 'I think I've played enough cards for this evening – what say we call it quits?'

'Always quit when you're in front, eh, Kate?' the man quipped light-heartedly as he too threw his cards down on the table. 'I think you're right though. I might go home and surprise my wife by having an early night.'

The second man at the table realized that the game was now over so he joined his companion in bidding the saloon-owner goodnight, and together they moved off towards the doors. As they approached the batwing doors, two men entered the saloon from the street. These two men stepped aside to let the townsmen out of the bar-room, and then stood looking around the room.

Kate remembered seeing them both earlier in the evening when they had entered the saloon and had stood looking around the bar-room in exactly the same manner – only that time they had turned and left without speaking to anyone. This time they walked across to where the last two townsmen in the bar-room were sitting playing checkers at a table, and drew their six-guns.

'You've got ten seconds to get out of here,' one of the two men demanded, and when neither of the townsmen at the table responded to this demand he spoke out again. 'I'm warning you that I'm going to shoot you at the end of ten seconds, so if you think I'm joking just stay there.'

The two men looked at each other, and then knocked the table over as they clambered to their feet and headed for the doorway. Neither of them looked back, not even when Kate Brown climbed to her feet and spoke out.

'What the hell do you think you are doing?' she demanded of the two gunmen. 'This is my saloon, and I'll say who is staying and who is leaving – and I think it would be a good idea if you left right now.'

One of the two gunmen walked across to face the saloon-owner, and the smile that he gave her caused a chill to run up her spine.

'I like a woman with spirit, but I don't have time for you now,' he warned her. 'I suggest you go to your room and stay there until I say you can come out.'

'Who the hell do you think you are?' she demanded. 'I'll have the sheriff arrest you if you don't leave the saloon this very minute.'

'I'm Tyler Hobden,' the man informed her. 'And I really don't have the time to play games with you, lady. So you have two choices – either go to your room now, or one of my men will take you there and tie you to your bed.'

The saloon-owner realized that this man meant what he had said, but she refused to give in to him.

'I've already warned you to leave my saloon – now you've forced me to do something about it,' she proclaimed as she turned to face the men at the bar. 'I'll give any man ten dollars who will go and fetch the sheriff for me.'

The men at the bar seemed amused by this offer and when none of them moved to take up the offer, she turned her attention to the barman.

'Go and get the sheriff for me, Thomas,' she instructed, and the barman instantly started to move off along the bar towards the end.

A shot from a six-gun rang out inside the saloon and the large wall-mirror behind the bar disintegrated into pieces when the bullet struck it just inches from the barman's head. He instantly stopped moving and raised his hands in the air before looking across to where Hobden was standing with a smoking weapon in his hand.

'I told you that I don't have time to play games, lady,' the outlaw leader growled angrily. 'Gordon, take her to her room and tie her to her bed – and take all her clothes just to make sure she stays there.'

'You animal,' Kate declared angrily. 'If you

think I'm going to let that creature lay a hand on me you've got a lot to learn.'

Hobden locked eyes with the saloon-owner and once again felt his blood begin to pulse through his veins. He found her to be very attractive, and her green eyes only served to increase the attraction he felt for her. He realized that he didn't want the other men anywhere near her so he quickly changed his instructions.

'You can keep your underwear, and your barman can tie you up and collect your clothes,' he told her. 'But if I find that any of the ropes are loose, or if he leaves any clothing behind in your room, I'll shoot him. Gordon, take her and the barman upstairs to her room and wait outside the door until he has finished.'

The red-headed outlaw did as he was bid, and drew his six-gun before escorting the woman and the barman to the stairs.

Hobden stood silently and watched her climb the stairs, before he was able to turn his attention back to the men waiting for him at the bar. He then set about picking the men for the positions he had outlined to them back at the sheriff's office. When Tod Gordon rejoined them in the bar-room, Hobden told him that he would be in charge of the four men on the upper floor of the saloon. He also warned him that they were not to fire their weapons until he had fired the first shot, and that he would kill anyone who was foolish enough to disobey this order.

The men then broke off into their designated groups and took up their places as directed. Hobden moved around to each of their positions inside the saloon and checked their line of fire on the street, before then heading off across the street with the gunman he wanted to position in the building opposite the saloon. He kicked in the front door of the grain-store that was housed in the building, and climbed the stairs to the upper floor.

'Your job is to fire down on the posse if they happen to take cover on the other side of the street,' he instructed the gunman. 'But don't fire until you hear me fire first, and then make sure that you hit them when you do fire.'

'What happens if they take cover over on this side of the street?' the gunman asked.

Hobden shook his head in disgust and began to wonder if he had chosen the right man for the job. 'You use that little brain of yours and go downstairs and shoot them through the window on the bottom floor,' he advised him caustically before turning and leaving the room.

The outlaw leader then returned to the saloon and told the men to settle in for what could be a long wait. He took up position at the window on the lower floor next to Wilby Dixan. He had deliberately chosen to stay close to his companion because if the ambush went off as planned, he then intended killing Dixan and keeping the money from the Mitchell Wells bank job all for himself.

'You keep watch for a couple of hours while I get some sleep, and then I'll take over from you,' he instructed Dixan, who nodded his compliance without comment.

ELEVEN

The heat of the day had yet to settle in and the air was still cool as the four horsemen pushed their mounts along at an easy canter. The two riders at the rear of this group were leading four pack-horses that had bundles tied across their saddles, and even at a distance these bundles could be seen to have human form.

'I hope we get these bodies into a town and signed over to the local sheriff before the heat gets to them,' Sam proclaimed to Bob Ward, who was riding along beside the youngster leading two of the horses that were carrying bodies.

'We should reach the town of Logan soon,' the farmer informed him casually.

Suddenly Tate Sharp held up his hand and all four men reined in their mounts. 'Can you see that horse and rider waiting in amongst those bushes up ahead?' he asked.

Duke Baxter pulled his binoculars out of his saddle-bags and focused them on the distant bushes. 'Damn, you've got good eyesight, old-timer,' he quipped lightly as the man on the horse came into focus. 'What do you reckon he's doing waiting in those bushes?'

'I don't have a clue,' Tate confessed. 'But it might be a good idea if I rode on ahead to see what he's up to.'

His three companions didn't bother to argue with this proposal, and the old bounty-hunter pushed his mount into a gallop along the trail. He hadn't covered fifty yards towards the distant bushes before the rider broke from his cover and sped away towards the town of Logan at a fully stretched gallop. Tate Sharp instantly pulled his mount to a halt and waited for his companions to catch up.

'That was an interesting reaction,' he declared as they stopped next to him. 'I think we're going to have to be very careful from here on in to the town.'

The four men then started their mounts off along the trail once again, and they soon had the buildings of the small town of Logan in their sights. They quickly pulled off the trail into the cover of some bushes and viewed the town from a distance.

'Maybe we should enter the town separately,' Duke Baxter suggested. 'Hobden might be over there waiting for us.'

'You may well be right,' Tate agreed pensively. 'The way that rider acted back there when he saw us, I'd say there is something being planned for us in Logan.'

'If Hobden's not there we'll be wasting a lot of time by doing it this way,' Sam declared restlessly.

'Better to be sure than sorry,' Bob Ward warned him.

The youngster bit back his impatience and waited while Duke and Tate worked out the details of their entry into the town. Sam and Duke were to work their way around to enter the town from the north, while Tate and Bob would enter it from the south with the horses that were carrying the dead outlaws. The youngster was glad to be rid of the two horses that he had been leading all morning, and was even more pleased to be riding with Duke Baxter, a man whom he had come to admire greatly.

Tyler Hobden watched the horse-rider pull his mount to a halt outside the front of the saloon, and guessed that his quarry had finally arrived.

The man rushed into the bar-room and stopped in front of the outlaw leader. 'They're here,' he warned. 'There's four riders coming in from the south, and they'll be here soon.'

A rare smile twisted Hobden's lips as he took in this news. He was going to make these possemen pay dearly for the annoyance they had caused him at the Vidlers' cabin, and he was going to do it in style.

'Did they see you?' he asked suddenly.

'No, not at all,' the man lied quickly. He knew that he had waited too long before heading back into town, and that the

110

possemen had spotted him – but he had no intention of telling the outlaw leader of this mistake and then facing his wrath.

'Okay, put your horse around the back of the saloon with ours, and then come back in here with your rifle,' Hobden instructed him. The outlaw leader then sent Wilby Dixan off upstairs to warn the men that the posse was on its way in, and he also sent a second man to pass the same message to the gunman positioned across the street.

Within minutes all the men were back in position and watching the street keenly. The minutes seemed to drag like hours, but finally the sound of horses moving along the street from the south could be heard.

'Where the hell are the other two?' Hobden growled when he saw there were only two horse-riders coming into view. The outlaw leader frowned deeply as he tried to work out where the other two possemen could be, but the sound of a rifle being fired from the upstairs window of the saloon broke into his deliberations. On hearing this rifle-shot, both riders slid to the ground and used the cover offered by their horses to run for the refuge of a water-trough that was positioned on the other side of the street.

Hobden's temper exploded when he saw

that the two men had made it safely into cover, and he fired his rifle at their position in frustration. The rest of the gunmen in the saloon also began firing on the possemen, but it was all too late to hope for any success. The outlaw leader fired his rifle until it was empty, before then throwing it aside and standing back from the window.

'I'm going to kill the person who fired that rifle,' he growled as he turned and headed for the stairs. Stopping at the bottom, he turned back to face the men over at the window. 'Wilby, send one of the men out the back to see if he can get a clean shot at those two possemen from the alleyway at the side of the saloon. The rest of you keep them pinned down behind that water-trough, or your lives won't be worth living.'

The outlaw leader then quickly climbed the stairs and disappeared from view. He marched along the passageway and stormed into the first room he came to. 'Who fired the rifle?' he demanded.

The two gunmen at the window looked around and both of them shook their heads. 'It was someone next door,' one of them divulged quickly.

Hobden then turned on his heels and walked out of that room, and entered the next one. This room was bigger than the other one, and there were three men firing rifles out of the two windows that faced the street.

Tod Gordon, the leader of the local gunmen, looked around to see Hobden standing at the door with his six-gun in his hand. No words were spoken between them, but Gordon knew why the outlaw leader was there and he indicated the gunman beside him with an incline of his head.

Hobden stepped forward and pressed the muzzle of his six-gun against the back of the gunman's head. 'What's your name?' he asked, and the gunman tried to look around at the outlaw leader without moving his head.

'Josh Cantel,' he answered in a voice that showed the fear that he was feeling. 'I'm really sorry that I fired first, Mr Hobden – but it was an accident.'

'Not as sorry as you're going to be,' Hobden pronounced, before pulling the trigger of his sixgun. The gunman fell to the floor dead at the outlaw leader's feet, but this didn't seem to even register on Hobden's mind as he turned to face Tod Gordon.

'Send one of your men up onto the

rooftop, and tell him to see if he can get a clear shot at those two men behind the water-trough,' he instructed before then turning and walking from the room before Gordon could reply.

Sam and Duke were just entering the outskirts of the town when they heard the first shots. The two men quickly drew their weapons and pushed their horses into a gallop towards the centre of the town. Rounding the bend in the street, they could see that Tate and Bob were pinned down behind a water-trough by gunfire that was coming from the saloon across the street. They pulled their mounts to a halt just as a gunman stepped out of an alleyway on their right and took aim at the two men behind the water-trough with a rifle. Both Sam's and Duke's six-guns fired at the same time and the man dropped lifeless to the ground.

'Let's get into cover,' the deputy sheriff suggested as the hostile gunfire from the saloon was turned onto them. The two men snatched up their rifles as they dismounted, and moved into the cover of the alleyway where the dead gunman lay.

'You stay here while I go around the back,' Duke Baxter directed Sam before heading off down the alleyway without waiting for the youngster to reply.

Sam took a quick look around the corner of the building and saw that Tate and Bob were still pinned down behind the water-trough. They were busy keeping their heads down and occasionally returning fire, but most of the gunfire was coming from the ambushers who were holed up in the old saloon that was standing further down the street to Sam's right.

On seeing movement at the window of the building behind his two companions, Sam took aim and waited until he saw the shape of a person's head at the window, and then the barrel of a rifle eased out through the opening and aimed in the direction of his two friends. The youngster fired his rifle once, grimacing with satisfaction when he saw the man's head disappear from view inside the building and the rifle fall out onto the boardwalk as his bullet found its target.

Tate Sharp looked back over his shoulder at the rifle, and then across at his young companion. He gave a single wave of his hand to convey his thanks to the youngster, before returning his attention to the men firing on him from across the street. He and Bob had ridden straight into the middle of the ambush some three minutes earlier, and he was glad that they had both made it to the safety of the cover offered by the water-trough without one or both of them being killed. The farmer had a bullet-graze on his right shoulder where the first bullet fired at them had nearly found its target, but it was a minor wound and he was now returning the ambushers' fire whenever he got the chance.

Several bullets thudded into the ground close by Bob Ward's legs, and he took a quick look over the edge of the water-trough to see where they were coming from. 'There's a gunman up on the roof of the saloon, and he's working his way along to the right,' he warned. 'If he makes it across to the roof of that building next door he'll be able to fire directly in on us behind the water-trough.'

'You keep an eye on the buildings behind us, and I'll organize something for our friend on the roof,' the old bounty-hunter instructed his companion. He then waved his hand to catch Sam's attention, before pointing to the area of the rooftop. The young bounty-hunter quickly nodded his head in reply, and turned back into the alleyway and disappeared from view.

Sam had heard the rifle-shots that were fired from the roof area, and realized that he would have to try to help his two companions. He hoped that there was no-one else hiding in the buildings on the opposite side of the street who might attempt to back-shoot Tate and Bob, but he knew that the old bounty-hunter would now have that possibility well covered. He worked his way to the end of the alleyway, and stopped to survey the open area at the back of the main buildings. There were several ramshackle sheds standing at the rear of the saloon, but there was no sign of anyone amongst these structures.

The building that Sam was standing near was right next to the saloon, and his plan was to gain access to its roof and then hopefully get a clear shot at the gunman who was firing down on Tate and Bob. Moving across to the back door of the building, he tried the door handle but found that it was securely locked and bolted.

'Damn-it,' the young bounty-hunter muttered to himself as he looked around for another means of gaining access to the roof. A narrow wooden ladder leaning against a nearby oak tree caught his eye, and he moved across to it. The ladder was old and weathered, but it seemed sturdy enough to be able to take his weight. Leaving his rifle against the tree trunk, he carried the ladder across to place it against the wall of the building. Realizing that it would be near impossible to climb the ladder while carrying his rifle, he decided to leave it behind as he started up towards the roof.

The climb was much more difficult than Sam had expected, and the ladder groaned under his weight as he edged closer to the top. On reaching the edge of the roof, he stopped and looked around to see if he could locate the gunman on top of the saloon, but his vision was obscured by the rise in the centre of the gently inclining roof. The youngster quickly climbed the last few rungs of the ladder and moved out onto the rooftop. He then dropped down onto his hands and knees and crawled across the tiles towards the rise in the centre of the roof. As he drew nearer he spotted the gunman hiding behind the fascia of the saloon watching the street below. Even as Sam watched, the gunman climbed to his feet and made ready to jump the gap between the two buildings. The gunman waited until there was a volley of shots fired from inside the saloon before running towards the edge and propelling himself across the gap between the two rooftops with his rifle still in his hand.

Sam waited until the gunman had landed on his haunches on the rooftop, before he climbed to his feet and levelled his six-gun on the man's chest.

'Throw the rifle aside and put your hands in the air,' the young bounty-hunter demanded.

The gunman instantly froze. He then threw the rifle aside as instructed, but made no effort to do the same with his holstered six-gun.

'You would be doing yourself a big favour by listening to me, kid,' the gunman challenged him. 'There's a reward of two thousand dollars on those hombres down there, and if you help me I'll share it with you.'

'I'm one of them,' Sam declared angrily, and the gunman reacted by making a futile attempt at drawing his six-gun.

The youngster fired his six-gun once and then watched as the gunman staggered backwards under the impact of the bullet hitting him in the chest. Those few steps took him to the edge of the roof, but he seemed not to realize this as he toppled over the edge and disappeared from view down into the alleyway between the two buildings.

Sam quickly moved across to the edge of the roof and looked down into the gap between the buildings, and saw the gunman lying in an untidy heap on the ground. He was showing no signs of movement, and Sam concluded that he had probably broken his neck when he had landed.

The young bounty-hunter then moved across to the fascia of the building and waved to Tate Sharp behind the water-trough. He saw just how dangerous the situation had been for his old partner and the farmer, and realized that they would have been sitting ducks for the gunman had he made it into position on the rooftop where Sam was now standing.

A noise behind Sam drew his attention, and he turned to see Duke Baxter climbing onto the roof from the ladder that he himself had used to gain access to the rooftop. While he waited for the deputy to join him, he replaced the spent cartridge in his handgun with a fresh one.

'Where have you been?' he asked as Baxter joined him at the front of the building.

'I was trying to find a way into the saloon through the back, but it was locked up tightly,' the deputy declared as he walked over to the edge of the roof and looked down into the gap between the buildings where the body of the gunman lay.

'You've been busy,' he stated casually.

'He was trying to outflank Tate and Bob so he could get a clear shot at them,' Sam explained. 'I'm just thankful that I got him before he could get into position.'

'You've done a good job,' the deputy sheriff assured him. 'What are you going to do now?'

Sam guessed that Baxter was testing him to see if he'd managed to come up with a plan. 'I was thinking of getting over onto the saloon roof to see if I can find a way down into the saloon, and then having a crack at those gunmen on the first floor who are firing on Tate and Bob.'

'That's a damn good plan,' the deputy sheriff commended him. 'I guess you won't mind if I join you?'

'Not at all,' the youngster assured him before jumping across the gap between the buildings and landing on the slightly inclined roof of the saloon with the grace of a cat. The deputy sheriff quickly followed suit, and the two men then moved off across the roof to look for a means of gaining entry to the building.

As they neared the hip of the roof they both spotted a wooden cover lying off to one side of a manhole that was positioned in the middle of the roof section. The two men quickly moved across to the hole and looked down into the darkened interior of the saloon. They were unable to see anything inside, but a ladder could be seen leading down into the darkness.

'I'll go down first,' Sam announced as he stepped across towards the edge of the manhole.

'Okay, but be careful,' Baxter agreed hesitantly. 'They may have someone watching the manhole from inside.'

Sam had already considered this possibility, and his plan was to drop down through the manhole to the floor below to make himself less of a target. He lowered his legs over the edge before dropping into the darkness of the saloon below and landing heavily on the floor with a jolt that drove the air from his lungs.

Breathing deeply to regain his breath, Sam lay motionless on the floor and waited for his eyes to adjust to the dim interior of the building. Shapes soon started to appear out of the gloom, and the youngster realized that he was lying on the floor of a wide passageway that ran the full length of the upper floor of the saloon. There were doors leading off on both sides of the passageway, and he guessed that they led to the rooms that were used for paying customers.

'Are you okay?' Duke Baxter asked from above, but the youngster didn't bother to reply to this as he climbed to his feet and edged along the passageway to the nearest door that led to one of the rooms that faced out onto the street. Stopping outside this door, he saw that it was slightly ajar so he pushed it open. The room was well lit by the sunlight that streamed in through the window, and he saw the body of a gunman lying on the floor near the window. Sam mused that one of his companions down in the street had very likely shot this man, but his musing was quickly pushed aside when he heard the sound of pounding horsehooves at the rear of the saloon. He ran from the room and burst through into the room on the opposite side of the passageway. On reaching the window he saw seven horses moving away at speed from the back of the saloon towards the open land to the north of the town.

'Damn you to hell, Hobden!' he shouted angrily after the outlaw leader as he realized that he had escaped him once again. He fired off several shots in the direction of the escaping gunmen through the open window, but it was all in vain as they were already out of handgun range.

'Now that's no way for a handsome young man to speak in a lady's bedroom,' a female voice admonished him gently from behind.

Sam instantly spun around and levelled his six-gun on the person who had spoken. He saw a woman sitting with her arms tied to the head of a large iron-framed double bed, and she was watching him with a smile on her lips. She was in her mid-forties, but even at that age she had a sexiness about her that made Sam flush with embarrassment. This was made worse by the fact that she was clad only in her underwear, and that her low-cut bodice was doing its best to free itself of her breasts.

'I–I–I'm sorry, ma'am,' he apologized hesitantly as he tried to drag his eyes away from her ample bosom. 'I didn't know you were in here.'

At that moment Duke Baxter entered the room and saw Sam covering the woman with his six-gun. He burst out laughing when he saw the embarrassed look on the youngster's face, and this served to make

Sam feel even more self-conscious. The deputy then quickly moved across to cut the ropes that held the woman's arms to the end of the bed, and then sat down next to her and kissed her fondly on the cheek.

'It's been a long time, Duke,' she smiled as she kissed him on the cheek in return. 'And I must say I'm very glad to see you.'

'It's been too long, Kate,' Baxter replied. 'Although I don't remember you ever entertaining men this young in your bedroom the last time I saw you.'

'You're a damn fool,' she laughed as she punched him good-humouredly on the arm. 'Although, if they were as handsome as this young man I might well be tempted.'

'I'll leave you here with your lady friend, Duke,' Sam announced quickly as he crossed the room towards the door. 'I'm going out to check on Tate and Bob.'

'I'll catch up with you later, Kate,' the deputy sheriff declared as he quickly climbed from the bed. 'I'd better make sure that we've flushed out all them outlaws before I sit down and chinwag with old friends.'

'I'll be waiting,' the woman called after him. Then quickly added, 'Even better – send that young man back up here to me.'

TWELVE

Tyler Hobden rode along on his horse deep in thought, and the accompanying six horse-riders kept well clear of him as he pushed his mount along at a punishing pace. He was furious with the local gunmen for the mess they had made of the ambush on the posse, and he wanted badly to make someone pay for it. The whole plan had turned into a humiliating defeat for the outlaw leader, and he had been forced to escape out through the back door of the saloon in company with the inept gunmen who had destroyed his plan in the first place. His horse stumbled when it tripped on a clump of grass, and he abused it vehemently as it struggled to regain its balance.

'Maybe we should slacken our pace and save our horses a bit,' one of the riders shouted from behind, and Hobden savagely reined in his horse causing the following riders to swear loudly as they were forced to take evasive action to stop their mounts from crashing into him.

'You got something to say, Gordon?' the outlaw leader asked the red-headed leader of the local gunmen who had made the suggestion.

'I only thought that maybe we should slow down a bit to save our horses some,' the man replied nervously.

'Maybe you feel like taking over as leader of this group too?' Hobden pressed him.

'No,' the man replied quickly. 'But we did only agree to help you shoot those men that were following you – and not actually to join up with you and Wilby here.'

'And if you'd followed my orders and waited until those possemen were in position before firing, we wouldn't need to be running away like this,' Hobden declared angrily.

'It wasn't me who fired on them,' Gordon asserted in a defensive voice. 'It was Josh Cantel, and he's dead now so there's no use blaming me for it.'

'I don't blame you, Gordon,' Hobden replied amiably as his face relaxed into a friendly smile. 'I guess I was being a touch hard on you, and if you want to go your own way then it's all right by me.'

Wilby Dixan had heard his leader react

this way on many occasions before today where his voice changed from anger to amiable friendliness in a matter of seconds, and knew exactly what was coming next. He was positioned off to one side of the grouped riders, and he dropped his hand to his six-gun and eased the weapon from its holster.

'Can we have our money before we go?' Gordon asked.

'Yeah, of course you can,' Hobden replied as he made to reach back to his saddle-bags, but this movement turned into a quickdraw as the outlaw leader's hand came up with his six-gun in it. He fired three times at the other man, hitting him in the chest with each shot and killing him instantly. The noise of the gunfire spooked the dead gun-man's horse and it ran off with his limp body slumped over in the saddle. One of the other outlaws made a grab for his six-gun too, but Dixan shot him in the back before he could complete his draw. The three other riders tensed, but they quickly realized the futility of their situation and raised their hands in the air.

'You've got two choices,' the outlaw leader warned them. 'Either ride with me now and do as I say, or stay here and keep company with Gordon and his friend.'

The men looked at each other and finally one man spoke out on behalf of them all. 'We're with you, Hobden.'

Hobden then began to whistle cheerfully as he led the men off along the trail, once again at ease after feeling the power he held over other men's lives.

Impatience gnawed at Sam's composure as he waited for one of his companions to respond to the advice given to them by the sheriff of Logan. The four men were seated at a table located some six feet from where Sam was sitting at the bar, and he found himself biting back the urge to voice his opinion to the lawman. He had a half-full glass of foaming beer in his hand, but showed little interest in it as he waited restlessly for one of his companions to reply to the advice that the lawman had just offered them.

Duke Baxter reached across to refill the whiskey glasses of the other three men, before answering. 'I think your suggestion has merit, Morgan, but me and my friends here have a strong personal reason for going after Hobden.'

'You've already told me all that,' the sheriff

insisted. 'And I've warned you that Hobden will kill you all before you get anywhere near him. You've got yourselves a nice reward coming for those other outlaws that you brought in, so why don't you just let Hobden be and go home and enjoy that money before you get in too deep?'

'It sounds to me as if you want Hobden to go free,' Tate proclaimed calmly as he took a sip from his glass.

The sheriff's face reddened with anger and he stiffened in his seat as he answered. 'If you're too damn stupid to listen to good advice then it's your own fault – but don't you dare accuse me of being in with Hobden.'

'Well, it does seem a mite suspect when a killer like Hobden can set up such an elaborate ambush right here in the middle of your town, and you don't show your face until well after it's all over,' Bob Ward declared in one of his rare shows of speaking his mind.

'Damn you,' the sheriff snarled angrily as he grabbed for his holstered six-gun – but he froze mid-action when he saw that three other six-guns were already levelled on him well before he had completed his own draw.

Bob Ward's face turned a deep red, and he

climbed to his feet and reached across the table to grab the sheriff by the shirt-front. 'If you want to fight me, then fight me with your fists, you gutless rattlesnake,' he growled as he dragged the sheriff across the table like a rag doll. The table legs broke under Stratford's weight, and he cried out like a frightened child as he was dragged up to eye level by the enraged farmer.

'I don't have any time for low-life scum who could rape young girls and murder harmless old men, and I've got even less time for crooked lawmen – so I warn you to stay well out of my sight or I'll rip you into small pieces and feed you to the coyotes,' Bob Ward snarled before throwing the lawman backwards across the room to land in an untidy heap at the base of the bar.

The sheriff climbed to his feet and headed straight for the front door of the saloon. 'You will regret doing that to me,' he warned, before finally disappearing out through the batwing doors.

Bob Ward stood motionless with his arms hanging at his sides and shook his head sadly. 'I'm sorry about that,' he apologized to his companions. 'I guess I'm just a damn idiot who deserves to get his fool head blown off.'

'You only said what we were all thinking,' Duke Baxter assured the farmer.

'And that's the truth, Bob,' Tate testified with a grin on his face. 'It's just that you've got a more eloquent way of expressing yourself than we have.'

This taunt served to put everyone at ease, and the men laughed easily as they moved across to the bar where Sam was still seated on a bar-stool.

'We'll need another bottle and some fresh glasses,' Duke Baxter announced as he vaulted over the bar and collected a bottle of whiskey from the shelf and placed it on the bar next to three clean shot-glasses.

Some twenty minutes had passed since Sam and Duke had descended the stairs to the bar-room to find that Tyler Hobden and his surviving gunmen had all managed to make a clean break for it. While the youngster had gone out to inform his two older companions that the building was now secure, the deputy sheriff had returned upstairs to help Kate Brown to find some clothing.

The four men had then gathered back in the bar-room, and were discussing the ambush when Sheriff Morgan Stratford entered the building from the street. To their

surprise the lawman seemed totally unconcerned about the fact that a wanted outlaw
had managed to set up an ambush right in
the middle of his town – and they were even
more surprised when he went on to try to
convince them to give up their pursuit of the
outlaw leader.

'When are we going after Hobden?' Sam
asked impatiently.

Tate took a pensive sip of his whiskey
before answering the youngster's question.
'I think we should take a bit of time and
think over our plan of attack. Hobden is like
an angry rattlesnake at the moment, and we
should be well advised to ease the pressure
off him before he decides to turn on us
again and do us some real harm.'

'You mean you're taking the sheriff's
advice?' Sam asked incredulously.

'Hell no,' his companion chuckled. 'But
Hobden has shown that he will turn back
and have a go at anyone who trails him too
closely, so common sense tells us to try a
different means of attack.'

'He's right, Sam,' Duke Baxter asserted.
'There is no sense in pushing him too far
too soon.'

Sam could see the sense behind the plan,
but was still impatient to be on the outlaws'

trail. He sipped at his drink and thought deeply about the problem until movement at the top of the stairs caught his eye.

The lady owner of the saloon was standing on the upper landing looking down at the men at the bar, and her beauty once again caused Sam to feel a constriction in his chest. She was now wearing a long, flowing, red-coloured gown that incorporated a plunge neckline that clearly showed her ample bosom.

'Come down and join us, Kate,' Duke Baxter demanded, and she readily obeyed by descending the steps and crossing to the bar where the men were standing.

'I owe you gentlemen my heartfelt thanks,' she declared gratefully. 'If you hadn't driven that monster away when you did, God only knows what would have happened to me.'

'I'd say Hobden would have been the one in danger,' Tate professed, drawing an instant frown from the saloon-owner.

Suddenly her frown disappeared and she beamed a smile as she stepped forward and wrapped her arms around the old bounty-hunter's neck and kissed him fondly on the cheek.

'It's been years since I last saw you, Tate Sharp,' she declared as she held him at arm's length and studied his features closely. 'You still look as old as the hills, and just as badly weathered.'

'You really know how to win a man's heart, Kate Brown,' he laughed easily. 'But what the hell are you doing in a backwater town like this anyway – and what has happened to that husband of yours?'

'The rattlesnake ran off and left me here about fourteen months back,' she explained. 'So I decided that this town is as good as any other, and after a lot of hard work I now own this saloon.'

'What kind of work pays that much money?' Sam queried innocently, but this question only served to cause his companions to burst out into laughter.

'A gentlemen should never ask a lady where she gets her money from, young man,' she admonished him lightly, and then gave him a smile that once again caused him to colour with embarrassment.

'What's this local sheriff got to do with Hobden?' Tate asked as the mood changed to more serious matters.

'I think they're working together,' Kate replied as she accepted Duke Baxter's assistance to climb up onto a bar-stool beside Sam. 'The men in the upstairs rooms didn't seem to realize that I could hear everything they said to each other during the night, and I heard a couple of them discussing how they had been asked by Sheriff Stratford to work for Hobden.'

'Did you hear anything else?' Baxter asked her.

'They planned to head for the old abandoned mining-camp located in the Red Hills to the north of here to hide out for a while. They thought that after killing you gents the law would be out in force looking for them, so they wanted a safe hideout to use until the heat had eased off them again.'

'I know that mining-camp, and believe me it's impossible to approach it without being seen,' Duke Baxter informed them. 'Red Hills is a collection of rocky hills sitting in the middle of a large flat plain to the north of here, and there's a couple of cabins built around a fresh-water spring in the middle of them. All Hobden needs to do is place a lookout on the highest of the hills, and he would have a three hundred and sixty degree view of the whole surrounding plain.'

'It sounds as if we're going to have to wait until they come out of there again,' Bob Ward proclaimed.

'You could be right,' Tate concluded.

'It could be a long wait,' Duke Baxter stated. 'Maybe we should head home and give up trailing Hobden for now.'

'No way,' Sam growled angrily. 'I'll wait until hell freezes over before I'll give up trailing him.'

'I'm with you, Sam,' Bob Ward declared.

'It was just a thought,' the deputy sheriff offered in his own defence.

'We should discuss it later after we've had a chance to give it some thought,' Tate directed his companions. 'But for now we will have to go and find Stratford and try to stop him from getting word to Hobden about us.'

'He lives in the sheriff's office down the street to the right, and he keeps his piebald gelding at the old livery barn up the street to the left,' Kate informed them. 'Now you gents go and find him, while me and this young man stay here and get to know each other some more.'

'I'm going with you,' Sam announced, and quickly sprang to his feet before heading for the front door followed by the raucous laughter of his companions. He waited outside the saloon for them, and once they'd joined him they split up into two groups and headed off in opposite directions. Tate and Bob headed to the right towards the sheriff's office, while Sam and Duke headed towards the old livery barn. There were people already moving around the street now that the shooting was over, but most of them gave the youngster and the deputy sheriff a wide berth once they saw the hardened look they had in their eyes.

'You weren't really serious about giving up the hunt for Hobden, were you?' Sam asked the deputy sheriff.

'No, not really,' Baxter replied easily. 'But you must always remember that sometimes you don't get your man, and you may have to be satisfied to settle for less than what you first hoped for.'

Sam didn't bother to reply to this comment, but his mind worked over it as he moved along the street. He had a lot of respect for Duke Baxter, and realized that the deputy sheriff had years of experience behind him that he himself could only hope to attain, but he still felt that to give in to a person like Tyler Hobden was practically the same as sanctioning the crimes that he had committed.

'That's the livery barn across the street,' Duke Baxter announced, breaking into the youngster's thoughts. 'You wait here while I head around the back, and then you move in through the front entrance – but be careful.'

The deputy sheriff then headed off across the street and disappeared through the stockyards that were built between the side of the livery barn and its neighbouring building.

Sam counted out one hundred seconds before crossing the street and then warily entering the front of the livery barn. It was very dark inside, and the youngster stopped just inside the door and waited for his eyes to adjust to the dim interior. He then moved off down the aisle that ran through the centre of the stalls in search of the piebald gelding that belonged to the sheriff. He was halfway down the aisle when he spotted the horse penned in a stall off to his left.

Moving across to the gate of the stall, Sam looked the horse over. There was no sign that anyone had attempted to saddle the horse recently, and the youngster spotted a dust-covered saddle still hanging over the wooden rail at the front of the stall. This dust showed that it hadn't been used for some time, but it didn't mean that it wasn't going to be used soon though. Sam kept this in mind as he turned and made to move off towards the back of the livery barn in search of the rogue lawman.

'Don't move and I won't be forced to kill you,' a voice instructed Sam from the darkness of one of the stalls.

The youngster instantly froze as instructed, but moved his gaze around in an attempt to locate the source of the voice. The local sheriff stepped out of a stall further back in the stables, and Sam saw that he had his six-gun in his hand and that it was levelled on him.

'I was looking for you,' Sam informed him easily. 'Tate and the others gave some more thought to your advice on Hobden, and want to speak to you.'

'I'm not so stupid as to believe that they have changed their minds, kid,' the lawman growled in return. 'And I'd have been well gone by now if I hadn't have gone back to my office for my belongings.'

'I think you would be better off coming with me,' Sam pressed him. 'We won't let you get to Hobden and warn him about us.'

'You won't have a choice, kid. I'm leaving this place as soon as I saddle my horse, and you will be my insurance that they don't try anything.'

'You don't really think that I'm going to let you use me as a hostage, do you?' Sam scoffed. 'I don't have much time for crooked lawmen, but I'm giving you a chance to give yourself up now and live before you get in too deep and dig your grave even deeper beside Hobden.'

The lawman was now sweating profusely, and the six-gun he was holding was unsteady in his hand. 'You think you know everything, don't you, kid?' he chided. 'Well, you might like to learn that life isn't as black and white as you'd like to think it is, and that people aren't always as pure as they seem. You'd be shocked to learn that...'

A single shot exploded inside the livery barn, and a gaping third eye appeared in the lawman's forehead before he slumped to the floor dead. The bullet had come from directly behind him and hit him in the back of the head before exiting through his forehead.

Sam quickly palmed his six-gun and jumped into the cover of the nearest stall, and aimed his weapon in the general direction from which the shot had come. He couldn't see anyone in the darkened depths of the building, but visibly relaxed when he saw Duke Baxter step out of the shadows and move towards him.

'You can lower that now, I'm on your side,' the deputy smiled as he removed the empty shell from his six-gun and replaced it with a fresh one.

'Why the hell did you shoot him?' Sam asked irritably as he moved out from his cover. 'I'm sure he would have given himself up to us without a fight.'

'I don't take risks,' Baxter replied as he rolled the dead sheriff over onto his back with the toe of his boot. 'In my business you shoot to kill when your opponent has his gun out, or you will end up by having a very short career in this job.'

Sam bit back his irritation and turned and walked from the livery barn towards the street. He was annoyed that Baxter had shot the sheriff, but he also knew that he had done the right thing as he saw it.

Exiting the building, the young bounty-hunter saw Tate and Bob hurrying up the street towards him with their six-guns ready in their hands. On seeing him standing at the entrance to the building they slackened their pace, but both men arrived short of breath from their exertion.

'What was the shooting we heard?' Tate asked his young companion as he stopped outside the livery barn.

Sam explained what had happened, and then stayed outside while the other two men went inside to check on the dead sheriff.

THIRTEEN

'I still don't feel comfortable with this plan, but I guess there is no choice but to go ahead with it,' Baxter relented as he sat down next to Tate and Sam on the rooftop of the saloon. 'It's not that I think you're not capable of carrying it off, Sam. It's just that you'll be going up against a killer with a very unstable mind, and there's no way you can predict how he will react if you suddenly arrive at his hideout.'

'No-one can predict how Hobden will react,' Tate assured him. 'But he knows that we are on his trail, and it was only luck that saved me and Bob this time. We know that he will keep laying ambushes for us until he either kills all of us, or forces us to give up the chase. So we've got no choice but to change our plan of attack, and we can only hope that he accepts Sam as a harmless kid who is no threat to him personally.'

The deputy didn't put up any further argument and the three men went on to study the plain to the north of the town through a pair of binoculars. It was a sea of yellow grass that had the occasional patch of green where a stand of stunted bushes struggled to survive in the dry climate, but the distant hill-line that marked the plain's northern extremity was virtually bare of plant growth. It was agreed by the three men that this would be the most likely place where Hobden would set an ambush for anyone who tried to follow him. A small break in the hill-line could be seen through the binoculars, and it was through this break that the trail wound its way up into the hills and then on to the plains further to the north. These hills were too far away to see any real detail, but it allowed the two older men to explain to the youngster what he could expect once he left the plain and headed up into the hills.

The sun was very low in the sky when they finally came down from the saloon roof and made their way back to the bar-room. They found Bob Ward waiting for them, and the three men joined him at his table. They then went on to discuss their plan in more detail, and Baxter continued to express his doubts whether Hobden would allow Sam to enter his hideout without suspecting his motives. These doubts remained unresolved, but they were put aside as the men sat down to their evening meal. While they were eating their food, Kate Brown joined them at their table and gave each of them their room-keys. Sam was speechless when the attractive saloon-owner passed him his key and pointed out that his room was located right next door to hers. She then gave him a broad wink before heading back towards the bar, leaving the youngster to suffer the taunts of his companions.

After the kidding had abated, Tate Sharp came up with a suggestion that Sam quickly accepted. 'I will take your room tonight and you can take mine. Then we can be sure that you get plenty of sleep in readiness for tomorrow,' the old-timer proposed.

'Don't we get to draw straws for this job?' Duke Baxter asked lightly.

'No, not this time,' Tate asserted with a grin. 'You couldn't pay me enough to miss seeing her face when she come into the room and finds me there instead of this young buck.'

All three older men laughed loudly at this,

but Sam sat quietly, deep in thought. He was flattered by the older woman's interest in him, but his heart was still with the young girl who was staying at Bob Ward's farm many miles away to the south of where he now sat, and she was the only female that he was interested in.

It was well over one hour later whilst the four men were playing poker at the table that Duke Baxter suddenly came up with his idea. 'Why don't we put a little show on for Hobden's benefit tomorrow, and it might help to make Sam's entry into his hide-out a little easier?' he suggested with a grin on his face.

'What do you mean, a little show?' Sam asked doubtfully.

'It will all depend on whether we can find a local man to help us make up the numbers, but I think it might well work,' the deputy informed his companions. He then went on to explain his plan in detail, and their card-game was quickly forgotten as they discussed it at length.

It was just after nine o'clock when the deputy called the saloon-owner over to ask her if she knew any local man who would be willing to help them out, and she suggested her barman who had reappeared after being found locked up in the cellar under the saloon. They then finalized their plan before heading for their rooms and bed. As Sam stood up from the table he received another lecherous wink from the shapely saloon-owner, and this convinced him that he would be much safer in his old partner's room than in the one she had selected for him. Once inside the room he quickly locked the door, and as an afterthought dragged a straight-backed chair across and jammed it up under the door handle for added security.

The next morning Sam was woken by Bob Ward knocking on his door and calling out his name. Climbing from his bed, he crossed the room and moved the chair aside before opening the door to allow the farmer to enter. 'Is there any sign of Tate yet?' he asked.

'Yep, he's downstairs getting breakfast,' the farmer informed him as he sat down on the straight-backed chair. 'And he's got a smile on his face that is wider than the Mississippi River.'

'Has he said anything about last night?'

'No, but I think Kate found a novel way of punishing him for finding him in your room.'

147

Sam chuckled at this remark as he set about packing his belongings into his bed-roll. He was conscious of Bob Ward watching him intently as he did so, but the farmer didn't speak to him until he had finished packing his bed-roll and had placed it on the floor near the doorway.

'I just wanted to say that I wish I was going with you this morning,' Bob informed him. 'I've never met this Tyler Hobden, but I would give my left arm to be able to spend five minutes in a room alone with him.'

'I wish you were coming too,' Sam declared. 'But I guess I will have to play this one alone for a few days until I find a way of getting to Hobden.'

'Just don't go taking any chances with him, son,' the farmer begged him. 'I know that you're pretty fast with that six-gun of yours, but to beat a man like Hobden you will have to be fast with your brain as well.'

'I'll keep that in mind, and thanks, Bob,' the youngster replied as he pulled the silver half-hunter watch from his shirt-pocket and began to rewind its mechanism.

'Did the girl give you that watch?' Bob asked, eyeing the timepiece in the youngster's hand.

'Yes,' Sam replied as he held it out for the

farmer to examine more closely. 'I know it sounds stupid, but it makes me feel as though she's here with me while I keep it in my pocket close to my heart.'

'That's not stupid, Sam,' Bob Ward assured him. 'Sometimes in life you meet people you instantly feel at ease with, and I believe this is a spiritual friendship. I'd say that you two have got that kind of friendship, and that it is something you should always value – even when you are apart.'

Sam merely nodded his head and silently considered the man sitting opposite him. Bob Ward was a giant of a man, but had a gentleness about him that made people instantly like him. He rarely spoke out, even when the others were in deep conversation around him, but when he did speak it was usually straight to the point and he would say exactly what was on his mind. He struck Sam as being a person who was slow to anger, but one to keep well clear of once his temper was aroused.

'How did you meet Tate?' Sam asked him,

The farmer looked at him and considered the question for a moment before answering. 'He was after my bounty,' he replied honestly.

This reply shocked Sam, and it must have

shown on his face because the farmer chuckled deeply before speaking again. 'I guess I don't look the criminal type, eh?'

'What'd you do that would cause the law to put a bounty on your head?' Sam asked after regaining his composure.

'I killed two men,' Bob answered slowly.

Sam shook his head in disbelief. He was dying to ask more questions on the subject, but he realized that the farmer had the right to privacy, and might not appreciate further discussion on the subject.

'Aren't you going to ask me who I killed?' Bob asked as if reading his mind.

'I thought you mightn't want to talk about it,' was the youngster's hesitant reply.

'It's not something I tell everyone I meet,' the farmer explained. 'In fact, I'm not at all proud of it – but then I'm not ashamed of it either.'

Sam simply nodded his head and waited for him to begin his explanation. He felt sure that there was something behind Bob's reasoning for letting him in on his past, and this soon became clear as the farmer began to speak.

'I was married to another girl long before I met Hope,' the farmer revealed slowly. 'We lived on a farm that my parents left me down in Louisiana. It was a great piece of land that fronted right onto the river, so we had a plentiful water-supply and rich alluvial soil that would grow just about anything. We lived there for four years and even built ourselves a new home, but then an old man and his two sons bought the cotton-farm that joined our land. At first they acted friendly and quite neighbourly, but that all changed after they offered to buy me out and I refused. It dragged on for several months, with him and his sons doing everything they could to force me to accept their offer, but I still refused. It all came to a head one day when the sons rode in and torched my home while I was away in town. My wife was home sick in bed that day, and she died in the fire.'

Bob Ward paused momentarily and took a deep breath to steady his voice before continuing. 'After coming home and finding her, I rode out and killed both of the sons with my bare hands. I don't really remember all that much of what happened that day, but I do remember standing over a broken old man who was grovelling in the dirt at my feet pleading for his life, when it suddenly dawned on me that I'd become as bad as him and his sons, and that I should have let the law make them pay for their crimes.'

Sam pondered on what he had just heard and realized that he himself had felt the same crazed need for revenge when he had started out on his hunt for Hobden and his men, but now he felt in control of that urge and only wanted to make sure that Hobden and his men were brought to justice and punished for their crimes.

'Did you go to jail for killing them?' he asked.

'Sort of,' the farmer replied easily. 'Tate went all the way back to Louisiana with me, and stood by me during my trial. I was kept locked up in jail during the trial, while Tate went out to find people who would testify about the threats that the old man and his sons had made to the other people whose land adjoined theirs. The jury found me not guilty of murder, but guilty of man-slaughter, and I was given a suspended jail sentence – so I guess you could say that I owe my life to Tate Sharp.'

Sam had never heard this story before about his old partner, but it didn't surprise him any. Tate Sharp was as tough as nails, but he had a heart as big as an ox on the inside. He would play the game by the rules that were set down by the person he was hunting, and if they wanted to play it hard he was ready to oblige.

'Well, I guess we had better go downstairs and get some food into us as it's going to be a long day,' Bob declared as he headed for the door, and Sam swung his bed-roll up onto his shoulder and followed him.

The two men made their way down to the bar-room where Tate and Duke were already seated at a table and eating breakfast. Sam bid them both good morning as he deposited his bed-roll on the floor beside his chair and then sat down next to his old partner. He eyed him questioningly for a moment with one eyebrow raised, but found it impossible to keep the smile from his face when he saw that the older man's eyes were red-rimmed from lack of sleep.

'You sleep well, Tate?' he asked in mock innocence.

'Not too bad,' the old bounty-hunter replied grumpily.

'That's good,' Sam replied easily. 'So I guess Kate wasn't too upset about not finding me in that room then?'

'Mind your own business,' Tate grumbled around a mouthful of eggs and hotcakes.

This reply brought about a burst of laughter from the other men at the table, but they quickly quietened down when the buxom saloon-owner entered the bar-room and walked across to their table carrying a couple of plates of food which she placed in front of Sam and Bob.

'Thanks, ma'am,' Sam said politely, but realized that she hadn't heard him speak because her attention was riveted on his old partner seated next to him. She stood gazing at the old bounty-hunter with a glazed look in her eyes for several seconds before turning away and heading back towards the kitchen.

'You've certainly left an impression on that lady,' Bob Ward declared after she had disappeared from view.

'She left an impression on me too,' Tate announced with a hint of a grin on his face. 'My back will never be the same again.'

FOURTEEN

Wilby Dixan lowered the binoculars and tried to pick out the distant cloud of dust with his naked eyes. It was nearing eight-thirty in the morning, and the outlaw had been watching the steadily approaching dust-cloud for the past ten minutes.

'Can you see what it is?' his companion asked.

'No, not yet,' Dixan reported as he put the binoculars back up to his eyes. 'It'll be another five minutes before it's close enough to see what's going on.'

His companion accepted this news irritably and sat back against a rock and waited. He and Wilby Dixan had spent an uncomfortable night on the rocky ridge that looked down on the plain that stretched away towards the town of Logan in the far distance. Their closeness to the town had only served to aggravate his displeasure, especially when he thought about the comfortable bed he had over there within easy reach.

'A man needs his brain examined,' he grumbled. 'I should just get on my horse and ride back into Logan.'

'You do that,' Wilby Dixan encouraged him. 'But I warn you that Tyler Hobden never forgets it when someone runs out on him, and he usually makes them pay for it.'

'Damn Tyler Hobden,' the gunman spat, but the fear he held for the outlaw leader caused him to settle back and wait without further comment.

The dust-cloud was now close enough for Wilby Dixan to make out the figures of five men on horseback approaching along the trail at a gallop. At first he thought all five riders were together in one group, but as they drew nearer he could see that it was a single rider being pursued by the four other riders. The sound of handgun fire could be heard coming from the pursuing riders, and the front rider lay flat out along his horse in an attempt to reduce the target area he offered to his pursuers.

'Get ready to use that rifle. It looks like that posse is going to ride right into our laps,' Dixan ordered his companion as he continued to watch the spectacle through his binoculars. Hobden had directed him to shoot anyone who tried to follow them, and

156

he intended to carry out this order if the posse came within range.

The front rider was close enough now for Dixan to see that it was a youngster with long blond hair riding a dun-coloured horse. Even as he watched, the young man pulled his horse into a skidding halt before dragging his mount around to face his pursuers. He then palmed his six-gun and fired at the oncoming riders causing them to rein in hurriedly. Two of the riders slumped in their saddles as his deliberate shots found their mark, and the other two riders quickly dismounted and dived for cover behind some nearby rocks – but by the time they were in position and ready to return his fire, the youngster was once again speeding away towards the ridge at a full gallop.

'Damn, he's a cool one,' Dixan remarked as he focused the binoculars onto the surviving members of the posse. They were now climbing back into their saddles, but their spirit had been completely broken by the surprise attack from the youngster, and after collecting the two horses carrying their wounded or dead companions, they headed back in the direction of Logan – seemingly no longer interested in continuing the chase.

'He's one brave kid, that one,' Dixan remarked aloud as he lowered his binoculars and saw that his companion was taking aim on the approaching rider with his rifle. Quickly grabbing the muzzle of the rifle, he stopped him from firing. 'You damn fool – if you shoot that kid after what he just did, I'll damn well kill you.'

'Tyler Hobden said we was to shoot anyone who tries to follow us,' the gunman complained.

'Tyler Hobden would have given a thousand dollars to see what I just saw down there. So I can assure you that he will want to meet this kid, and anyone who harms him will end up as coyote bait.'

'It's your decision,' the gunman pouted, but realized that Wilby Dixan might well just have saved his life.

The two outlaws watched the youngster stop his horse for a moment to look back at his defeated pursuers, and then start his horse up into the hill-line along the narrow trail. The trail passed within ten feet of the outlaws' hiding-place on the ridge, and they didn't even have to move position as they waited for the youngster to arrive. Both outlaws held their rifles in their hands ready for use just in case the kid decided to take a shot at them, but when he rode into view and saw that there were two rifles levelled on him he quickly raised his hands into the air.

'We don't aim to hurt you, kid,' Wilby Dixan assured him. 'We saw what you did down there to those hombres chasing you, and wanted a chance to talk.'

'A funny way to greet a person if you only want to talk to them,' the youngster growled with narrowed eyes.

'We're not the law,' the outlaw quickly assured him. 'In fact, we've been sitting up here waiting to ambush that posse, but it looks like you have saved us the trouble.'

'Can't say it was my pleasure,' the youngster replied caustically. 'But what's all this got to do with me?'

'Well, seeing you done us the favour of sending that posse off with its tail between its legs,' the outlaw explained, 'I thought we might be able to offer you the use of our hide-out for a while.'

'That's mighty obliging of you, mister,' the youngster declared. 'But I'm not too sure that I'm ready to go to ground just yet.'

Wilby Dixan thought for a moment before continuing. 'It could work out to be very profitable for you,' he offered. 'I ride with

Tyler Hobden, and he is offering a sizeable reward for the members of that posse. By my reckoning you have already earned yourself a thousand dollars by shooting those two possemen down there.'

'Now you're talking my language,' the youngster stated. 'Okay, I'll come with you now, but I warn you that I ain't going to hang around too long after I get that money.'

'That's fine by me,' Dixan smiled, feeling relieved that he had managed to talk the youngster around. 'What's your name, kid?'

'Sam Brady,' he replied easily.

The three riders rode along in single file with Sam in the middle. The trail they were following began to wind down from the high country towards a plain that stretched away to the north as far as the eye could see. A group of small red-coloured hills rose out of this plain, and Sam thought they looked like islands rising out of a lake.

'How much further is this hideout?' he asked irritably.

Dixan turned in the saddle and pointed to the group of hills off in the distance. 'It's over there in those hills, and we should be there within two hours.'

Sam had already guessed that these were the same hills that the saloon-owner in Logan had earlier mentioned to him as the place where Hobden was heading to hide out, but he had to continue to play the part of an impatient kid to keep the outlaws from suspecting him.

Wilby Dixan had been accurate in his estimate on how long it would take to reach the hideout, and just on two hours later they were following a narrow trail that wound its way in between two of the hills. The trail was deep in shadow due to the sheer rock walls that rose up on both sides and blocked out the sun, and the surrounding rocks were a deep red in colour. After ten minutes of winding their way along this trail, they broke out into an open area that was a lush green pasture of several acres in size. In the middle of this pasture were four mud-brick cabins positioned around a single larger wooden building, and Wilby Dixan led the way directly towards them.

Two men emerged from this larger building and stood out in the open watching their approach. Sam studied these men closely as he approached, and sensed they were very interested in his arrival at the hideout. One of these men was short and fat, but his clothing was well-tailored and stylish. The second man was more of an average build, and his clothes were grubby and ill-fitting.

Sam and the two accompanying outlaws drew their horses to a halt in front of these men, and Wilby Dixan looked around warily before speaking. 'Where's Tyler?' he asked.

The short fat man eyed Sam over, and blatantly ignored the outlaw's question as he went on to ask one of his own. 'What's the kid doing here?'

'He's here to see Tyler,' Dixan explained coolly as he slid down from his horse and walked off into the building in search of the outlaw leader.

'Pretty young thing with that yella hair, ain't he?' the fat outlaw leered sickeningly, and received a snigger from the man standing beside him in return. 'Why don't you get down off that horse and come inside with me, youngster? I promise I'll look after you personally.'

A shiver ran up Sam's spine, and he felt repulsed by the sight of the obese creature standing before him. He had received taunts before in his life from other men about his youthful appearance and supposedly good looks, but this was the first time he had actually felt physically sickened by the person taunting him.

'I think I'm quite happy up here for the moment, thank you, mister,' he replied coolly.

The outlaw laughed sarcastically and contempt showed in his eyes as he spoke. 'You think you're too good for us, do you, Goldilocks?' he sneered. 'Maybe you should run off home to your mammy before you get scared some more.'

Sam realized that the man was now acting tough in front of his companion in an attempt to cover the embarrassment caused by being rejected. He saw that the fat man's gun-belt was greased and low-slung for a quick draw, and knew that excess body fat counted for very little when it came to speed of hand and straight shooting.

On noticing that Wilby Dixan and another man had emerged from the building, Sam swung his leg across the saddle and dropped to the ground beside his horse. He then beat the dust from the legs of his trousers before finally turning to look at the fat gunman again. 'I got no quarrel with you, mister,' he explained coolly. 'I just came here to see Tyler Hobden, and once that's done I'll be on my way.'

'A pretty boy with yella hair and a yella

spine to go with it, eh?' the fat man scoffed.

Sam recalled the many pieces of advice that Tate Sharp had given him about controlling the situation instead of letting the situation control you, but the part he was now playing as a tough young kid with a gun meant that he had no choice but to stand up to this man.

With the decision finally made, Sam locked eyes with the fat outlaw and smiled amiably. 'I bet you still suckle on your mammy's breast – that's why you're so bloated,' he goaded.

'You snotty-nosed little brat,' the outlaw snarled and grabbed for his six-gun.

Sam's response was well-practised and controlled, and his draw was smooth and fluid. His six-gun was levelled well before that of his opponent, and he fired a single shot at the fat outlaw, killing him instantly. The bullet hit the outlaw in the middle of the chest, and he dropped to the ground into an untidy heap. The man who had been standing beside the fat man also went for his six-gun, but Sam was ready for him and fired at him twice. This man staggered backwards under the impact of the bullets, and his six-gun dropped from his hand as he clutched at his chest. He too fell to the ground dead, but Sam hadn't seen this because he had already moved aim to cover Wilby Dixan and the man standing beside him at the front of the building.

'It's all your fight, son,' the man beside Dixan quickly assured him. 'And we've got no intention of joining in.'

Wilby Dixan and the man who had spoken moved across to where Sam was standing. The youngster instantly knew this man to be Tyler Hobden, and realized that the hand-drawn sketches he had seen of the outlaw leader on the Wanted posters had been pretty close to the mark.

'I'm impressed by the way you handled yourself there, kid,' Hobden declared as he eyed Sam. 'I was planning on killing that fat pig and his brother myself before the day was out, so you saved me the trouble.'

'Was he one of your men?' the youngster asked.

'Hell no,' Hobden chuckled. 'He ran this joint with his brother, and made his money by charging everyone a fee to stay here. He had a reputation for being very quick with his six-gun, but you made him look damn ordinary.'

'I can look after myself,' Sam asserted as he met the outlaw leader's unwavering gaze.

'Your man here told me that you would pay me a reward for those possemen I shot?'

'That's right,' the outlaw leader assured him. 'But I'd like to hear a bit more about your run-in with that posse before I pay you. Is there any problem with that?'

'Not at all,' Sam replied with a shrug of his shoulders.

'Look after the kid's horse, and then go up and relieve the lookout on the hill,' Hobden directed the man who had ridden in with Sam and Dixan earlier, and then led the way into the building.

On passing through the front doorway, Sam was surprised to see that the room was set up as a miniature bar-room; it even had a wooden bar built against the back wall. One of the tables was already occupied by one of Hobden's men, but he ignored Sam's presence and sat quietly sipping at his drink as the three men crossed the room to the bar.

'Get the kid a drink, Wilby,' the outlaw leader ordered his companion, who readily obeyed.

'I'll have a beer, thanks,' Sam instructed, and frowned when his request caused Hobden to burst out into laughter.

'You'll have what you're given, kid,' the

outlaw leader asserted after he stopped laughing. 'This may look like a saloon, but it serves red-eye whiskey and nothing else.'

'I guess I'll have a red-eye whiskey then, thanks,' Sam quickly corrected, and received a thump on the back from Hobden as he laughed out loud once again.

'I like you, kid,' he professed. 'You remind me a lot of myself when I was your age.'

Sam accepted this compliment from the outlaw leader by taking a deep breath to control his emotions. His skin crawled at being so close to Hobden, and he was tempted to draw his six-gun and shoot him dead – but he pushed this temptation aside. He instead made himself concentrate on his plan to wait until the opportunity presented itself to capture the outlaw leader, and to then take him back to Mitchell Wells to face the courts for his crimes.

'How safe is this place?' he asked as Wilby Dixan placed a shot-glass in front of him and filled it with whiskey.

'Safe enough,' Hobden replied, before emptying his shot-glass in a single gulp. 'We have a lookout up on that hill behind us, and he can see everything that moves for miles in any direction. He can give us an hour's warning that someone is heading in our direction, and if it's the law there are more than a dozen ways of getting out of here before they arrive.'

'It sounds safe enough,' Sam declared before putting his shot-glass up to his lips and gulping down its contents. The whiskey burned its way down his throat and threatened to incinerate his stomach-lining, and he burst out into a coughing-fit from the fire that raged in his throat.

Hobden and the other outlaws in the room laughed loudly at his reaction, and finally the outlaw leader thumped him on the back to help him regain his composure. 'Get the kid a drink of that water over there, Wilby,' he ordered.

The youngster took the glass from the outlaw and gulped the water down his throat noisily, and instantly felt an easing of the burning in his throat and stomach. He then placed the glass back on the bar-top and indicated that he would like a refill. Dixan obliged, and Sam finished off half the second glass of water before he could use his voice again.

'Thanks for the whiskey, but I think I'll stick with the water from now on,' he resolved, and this brought about a renewed burst of laughter from the outlaws.

'I'm sorry if I butted in on your plans by killing those two men out there, but they didn't leave me much choice,' the youngster explained.

'Never apologize to anyone for anything,' Hobden advised him. 'Anyway, you saved me the trouble of having to kill them myself.'

Sam saw the gleam that showed in Hobden's eyes when he talked about killing, and realized that the man was quite mad. Death and bloodshed excited him, and this made him much more dangerous than any crazed animal.

'Drink that water up, and then tell us about this posse you shot up,' Hobden demanded with the gleam in his eyes, and Sam did as he was bid and began relating the story about his concocted adventure.

FIFTEEN

Tate Sharp watched the light in the western sky fading away behind the clustered hills far off in the distance. His binoculars were of no further use now that the light was gone, so he returned them to their leather carry-case before relaxing back against the rock. He hoped with all his heart that his young companion was alive and safe at Hobden's hideout situated over amongst those hills, and that the outlaw leader hadn't managed to see through the story that the youngster had used to gain entry to his hideout.

A scuffling sound behind Tate drew his attention, and he turned to see Bob Ward moving up through the rocks towards him. He knew that the farmer was as worried about Sam as he was, and that waiting for sundown was as nerve-racking for him as it was for himself. Tate waited until Bob had settled down beside him before speaking.

'Did Duke get away okay?' he asked.

'Yes – and I hope he gets over there without being seen by Hobden's men,' the farmer replied. 'I reckon this next two hours will be the longest of my life.'

Tate merely nodded his head and mulled thoughtfully over their day so far. The three men, in company with the barman from Kate Brown's saloon, had managed to carry out the elaborate ruse that morning where they had played out the part of a posse chasing Sam in an attempt to capture him. Once they'd left the youngster to carry on alone, they had then headed back into town to get fresh horses and to kill some time before heading back out to see what kind of reception Sam had received from the outlaws. They had quickly found his tracks where he had halted to talk to the ambushers, and then where he had joined up with them to travel north to Hobden's hideout. All the signs seemed to point to the plan going off well, but there was no way of telling how Hobden had received the youngster once he had reached his campsite.

Bob Ward nudged Tate on the arm and pointed at something moving out in the gloom in front of them. The old bounty-hunter once again took out his binoculars and focused them on the area where the farmer had pointed, but he couldn't see anything out in the darkness. Tate knew that Baxter was out there somewhere moving towards Hobden's hideout, and that the next two hours were going to seem like an eternity while they waited for him to complete the next part of their plan.

The plan was for Baxter to move in on Hobden's hideout under the cover of darkness, and then to remove the lookout who was positioned on top of one of the hills. The deputy had assured his companions that it would be much safer for him to move in alone because he knew the layout of the hideout from a map he had once seen of the group of hills, and that he would need to move fast to be able to cover the distance to the hills before the moon rose in just over one and a half hours. Once the two-hour mark was reached, Tate and Bob would then move off and meet up with Baxter before moving in on the campsite where the rest of Hobden's gang was located. This meant that they were totally reliant on Duke Baxter to successfully carry out this part of the plan, or they might all end up dead after riding into a Tyler Hobden ambush.

Duke Baxter rode low on his horse and pushed it along at an easy gallop. He wasn't pushing his mount too hard, but it was still fast enough to be scary as they sped across the darkened landscape with little sight of what lay in front of them. Luckily his horse seemed to be able to sense the bushes and rocks that lay in their path, and it always managed to swerve aside just in time to miss these objects that loomed out of the darkness in front of them. On one occasion Baxter's luck seemed to momentarily desert him when his horse stumbled into a shallow wash-out that caused it to crash heavily to the ground. The deputy was thrown from the saddle, and the wind was knocked from his lungs when he too crashed to the ground. He lay where he had fallen for some time while he fought to regain his breath, and after several minutes climbed to his feet and retrieved his uninjured mount before continuing on.

Their pace was much slower after the fall, and Baxter gave a sigh of relief when the hills finally appeared in front of him. On reaching the base of the hills, he left his horse and moved off on foot in search of a track that he knew would lead him to the target he sought. The moon soon appeared over the horizon and the landscape became more illuminated, making it much easier for Baxter to make out the detail of the surrounding area. He soon found the narrow track that he was seeking, and began the laborious climb up its steep incline towards the crest of the hill.

Baxter swore to himself when his boot dislodged a stone that rolled away noisily down the slope of the hill. He squatted down on his haunches behind cover and waited to see if anyone had heard this noise, but when there was no challenge forthcoming he moved on once again. The narrow track that he was following was a game-trail used by the native animals when they came in at night to seek water in amongst the hills, and at the crest of the hill the track met up with a wider and more defined track. This wider track led off towards the top of the highest hill, and it was at the top of this hill that the deputy expected to find the lookout.

As Baxter reached the intersection of these two tracks he heard the sound of footsteps crunching on the gravel off to his left. He quickly sought the cover offered by a nearby bush and hunkered down beside the track. Finally a man appeared out of the darkness, and the deputy pulled a knife from his boot-top and waited patiently for him to approach. He cursed his luck at having arrived just as there was about to be a change of lookout, but realized that if he handled the next few minutes wisely, he would have two less outlaws to worry about later when he moved in on the campsite below.

Waiting until the outlaw had safely passed his hiding-place, Baxter then stepped out from behind his cover and clamped his hand over the man's mouth, while at the same time slashing his throat with the knife that he held in his right hand. The outlaw struggled momentarily in the deputy's grip, but quickly lost all sign of life as he slumped back into Baxter's arms. He then dragged the outlaw's body in behind some bushes and lowered it to the ground, before heading off to the right up the trail.

There were a couple of large boulders at the top of the hill, and Baxter stopped to survey the area. He could see a rough wooden shelter that was constructed between these boulders, and realized that this would be where he would find the lookout. He moved in closer to the shelter and was surprised when he wasn't challenged – but the sound of someone snoring from inside the shelter soon answered this question for the deputy.

The lookout was a very noisy sleeper, and Baxter felt annoyed that he had nearly killed himself by riding at breakneck speed across the open plain, only to find that the lookout had been asleep all the time. This irritation increased when Baxter moved up next to the entrance of the shelter and could smell the stench of stale whiskey in the air. The lookout wasn't just asleep, he was dead drunk and would have been incapable of seeing his own hand in front of his face, much less riders approaching across the plain in the moonlight.

'You don't deserve to live,' Baxter growled as he reached in and grabbed the man by the hair and pulled him up into a sitting position before slashing his throat with a single stroke of his knife.

SIXTEEN

It had been dark outside for some time when Sam looked up to watch the outlaw walk unsteadily from the room. The second outlaw had gone off some twenty minutes earlier to take over from the lookout up on the hilltop, but the replaced outlaw had yet to return to the bar-room.

Tyler Hobden was sitting across the table from Sam with a half-empty bottle in one hand and a glass in the other. He had been drinking steadily for the past two hours, and had thoroughly interrogated the youngster about the posse that had pursued him, as well as about his past life. He seemed to be amused by the youngster's brash manner, and showed an open friendliness towards him.

'What made you turn back and shoot up that posse?' the outlaw leader asked the youngster suddenly.

'If I didn't do something, they would have chased me until my horse dropped from exhaustion, and then used me for target practice,' Sam replied. 'So I thought it was a good idea to give them a bit of their own medicine to chew on.'

This reply brought laughter from both Tyler Hobden and Wilby Dixan, who was also sitting at the table. The two men were in a relaxed mood, and had been talking openly about their exploits in crime. Hobden was proud of the many robberies that he had managed to pull off over the years with his gang, but he readily admitted that the takings from the Mitchell Wells job were by far his best yet.

Sam felt sickened by having to listen to the two men boasting about the death and hardship they had brought to others, and finally he decided he'd had enough and needed a break from their company.

'I've got to go out and get my bed-roll off my horse and then find somewhere to sleep,' the youngster advised them as he climbed to his feet. 'Is it all right if I bunk down in one of those cabins out there?'

'Yeah, go right ahead,' Hobden encouraged. 'You'll find your horse in the corral out the back, and the best cabin is the far one on the north side of this building. When you're finished stowing your kit come back here and we'll have some food ready.'

Sam nodded his agreement and headed for the back door.

From his hiding-place, Duke Baxter watched the drunken outlaw stagger off towards some bushes a short distance from the front of the building. He saw him disappear from view and guessed that the man was going to use these bushes as a place to relieve himself. While the drunken outlaw was fully occupied, the deputy crossed from his hiding-place to the front of the main building and drew into the cover offered by the alleyway that ran between it and one of the cabins. The sound of voices could be heard coming from inside the main building, but this was quickly forgotten when he saw the drunken outlaw heading back towards him. Pulling his knife from his boot-top once again, Baxter waited until the man had passed him, before stepping out and grabbing him from behind. The practised action of clamping one hand over the victim's mouth whilst at the same time drawing his razor-sharp knife-blade across their throat had its intended result, and the outlaw struggled vainly in the deputy's grasp as he bled to death through the severed veins and arteries in his neck.

After dragging the dead outlaw back into the cover of the alleyway at the side of the cabin, Baxter headed for the larger building, hoping that he would find Sam alive and well somewhere inside the campsite.

Sam spread his bed-roll out on the bunk. He had found the cabin recommended by the outlaw leader to be passably clean inside, and with a smell about it that was at least tolerable. He was using a candle stub burning inside an old tin mug to work by, and the light it gave out was ineffectual and flickering. Three of the bunks already had bed-rolls spread out on them, and Sam was tempted to search through them in an attempt to find out something about his room-mates, but he knew that if he was caught doing such a thing he would be writing his own death-warrant.

Resisting this urge, the youngster sat down on his bunk and thought about the past hours he had spent talking to the outlaw leader. Their conversation had exposed very little about Hobden that Sam hadn't already known, but when the outlaw leader told him that he had been on the run from the law since he was sixteen years old, it showed that he was a hardened criminal with the cunning of a fox to be able to escape capture for that long. Sam was now even more wary of Tyler Hobden since seeing the insanity in his eyes when they had talked about death and killing, and he felt relieved that Hobden had taken him at face value on his arrival at the hideout, and had seemingly believed everything he had been told by the youngster.

Sam felt the need to climb into his bunk and sleep, but instead he crossed the room to the table and blew out the candle before heading for the cabin door. There was an uneasy feeling inside him that he couldn't quite put to rest, but he assumed it was caused by his close proximity to Tyler Hobden, and the fact that he wanted badly to make him pay for the pain he had caused Sarah. The memory of the girl caused Sam's heart to jump and he put his hand up to his chest to feel the half-hunter watch that was resting in his breast pocket. The touch of the watch against his chest gave him a warm feeling inside that spread throughout his body, and seemingly renewed his energy as he strode across the open ground towards the rear door of the main building where Hobden and Dixan were waiting for his return.

As Sam placed his hand on the latch in readiness to open the door, he heard his name spoken by someone inside the building. The young bounty-hunter strained his ears to listen, but it was only Hobden's voice that could be heard now and it clearly showed his anger as he shouted at someone else in the room. 'You let that damn kid come in here after me?' he demanded loudly. 'And I suppose you think you are going to get your share of the money now?'

There was a muted reply that Sam couldn't quite make out, so he quickly pulled his six-gun from its holster and moved across to a small window built into the back wall. The glass was dirty and badly stained from the candle-smoke, and he could only just see the three people standing inside the room. Hobden and Dixan were easy to recognize as they stood with their backs to the window, but the third person standing at the other end of the room facing the window was impossible to identify through the dirty glass.

Sam's true identity was now out and that meant that his life was in grave danger. He had the choice of making a run for it now, or attempt to capture the outlaws. The thought of running away from Tyler Hobden repulsed the youngster, so he settled on the second choice. He knew that the outlaws would be expecting him to enter through the back door – so he decided to head for the front door instead. He was only halfway down the side of the building when he heard the sound of a shot being fired from a handgun inside the building, which was immediately followed by two more shots.

Sam quickly covered the last few yards to the corner of the building and stopped beside the window that was built into the front wall. He looked in through the dirty glass of the window, and could see the shape of a man standing over two bodies on the floor of the room. He recognized this man to be Duke Baxter, and he smiled with relief as he stepped towards the front door – but stopped dead in his tracks as he realized that there was a good chance that he would get his head blown off if he burst into the room unannounced.

'I suppose I'd better warn him that it's me out here,' the young bounty-hunter muttered to himself before tapping on the half-open door several times with the barrel of his six-gun.

'Duke, it's me, Sam Brady,' he shouted,

and waited for the lawman to reply.

Baxter swung the door wide open and stood looking at the youngster. 'Where have you been?' he asked. 'I thought Hobden must have killed you.'

'I was over in one of the cabins laying out my gear,' Sam replied as he stepped past the deputy into the room. He saw Wilby Dixan and Tyler Hobden dead in the middle of the floor, but there was no-one else to be seen in the room.

This caused Sam to stop and look round at the deputy, but Baxter spoke first. 'How many men did Hobden have with him?'

Sam hesitated a moment, and realized that he was still in danger until all of the outlaws were accounted for. 'Well ... I saw three down here including Wilby Dixan, and I think he had one up on the hill as a lookout.'

'I've disposed of the lot, then,' Baxter assured him.

Sam walked across the room and knelt down next to the outlaw leader to examine the body. He saw that Hobden had been shot in the chest with a single bullet, and that Dixan had two wounds to his upper body. The words that he had heard spoken by Hobden when he was listening at the back door of the building came back into his mind, and he turned to look at the deputy.

Duke Baxter was standing by one of the tables with his hand resting on a set of bulging saddle-bags.

'You're one of them?' Sam asked incredulously.

'Hell no, Sam,' the deputy assured him. 'I was just making sure this was the money from the Mitchell Wells bank.'

'You're lying,' Sam accused him. 'I was standing at the back door and heard you talking with Hobden. You told him that I came in here after him, and he threatened that you weren't going to get your share of that money. That's why you killed him.'

Baxter shook his head and looked as if he was going to continue to deny this allegation, but instead gave a sigh and confessed. 'Okay, I was in on the bank hold-up with him, but I had nothing to do with any of the killings. He was supposed to just take the money and leave town, but I guess he enjoyed killing too much.'

'The fact that you helped him makes you just as bad as he was,' Sam accused angrily as he climbed to his feet to face the deputy sheriff. 'And I'm not letting you get away with it, so I suggest that you drop that six-gun now before I'm forced to make you.'

'Don't be silly, Sam,' Baxter warned. 'You know that I'm faster than you are, and that I won't just give in to you. So why don't you go back over to your cabin and forget that you saw me – and I'll give you a share of this money to take with you.'

This offer of a share in the money made Sam angry, but he forced himself to control his emotions as he faced up to the deputy sheriff.

'I'm not for sale, Duke,' the youngster declared. 'I'm going to take you back to Mitchell Wells to face the courts for your involvement in the bank hold-up - so I'm warning you to give up now.'

Baxter stepped clear of the table and faced up to the youngster. His face was expressionless as he stood eyeing Sam, but inside his mind was in a turmoil. He liked Sam Brady, and wanted anything but to have to kill him, but the youngster had a grim determination about him that was going to be hard to diffuse.

'Sam, you're forcing me to draw against you when it is the last thing I want to do,' the deputy beseeched. 'For God's sake let me leave with the money, and save yourself.'

'The only way you're going to walk out that door is as my prisoner,' the youngster insisted. 'But you can do me a favour by telling me what made you turn into the type of person who would get mixed up with a killer like Hobden – especially when you're a lawman?'

Baxter shook his head sadly, and took a deep breath to control his emotions. He was in a situation that wasn't to his liking. He wanted to get moving with the money as soon as possible, and this young bounty-hunter was all that stood between him and freedom, but he was at a loss as to how he was going to convince the youngster that he was committing suicide by attempting to stop him. Maybe if he told him what he wanted to know he would understand the reasoning behind his actions, he thought.

'Okay, Sam,' he relented finally. 'If you want to know what drove me to take up with the likes of Tyler Hobden then I'll tell you. I started my life just like you with grand ideas of what's right and what's wrong in life, and always dreamed of being a lawman to put these ideals into practice. I lived on pitiful wages as a deputy sheriff in towns that had more than their fair share of law-breakers, but I always stuck by my grand ideals. Even after I met a beautiful girl and fell in love, I still believed that honesty was the way to live life, and this meant that after we were married we could only afford to live in a ramshackle little cabin on the outskirts of town, and had barely enough money to buy food. Then one day I rode out with a posse in pursuit of a gang of outlaws, and while I was away a couple of drunken cowboys broke into my cabin at night and raped and killed my wife. When I got home she was already buried, and the two drunks were still free because the judge decided that they were too drunk at the time to be held responsible for their actions.'

A catch in Baxter's voice halted him for a moment, and he took a deep breath before continuing. 'I killed them both and then climbed on my horse and headed out of town. After that I started to take note that the crooks are the ones who always get the good breaks in life, and anyone stupid enough to have puritanical ideals and try to live them is an idiot who deserves to be treated like the damn fool that he is. So now you know what life is all about, kid – and that you are a damned fool if you don't take some of this money and set yourself up for the rest of your life.'

Sam felt sorry for the hurt that Baxter had experienced in his life, but he believed that if you let yourself be dragged down to the level of the crooks and criminals and those who preyed on other people, then life wasn't worth living. 'I'm sorry to hear about your wife, Duke,' he expressed sincerely. 'But you're totally wrong about it being okay to take advantage of folk just because other people do. It's selfish of you to think only about yourself, and not give a damn about the hurt that you inflict on other people. It makes you just as bad as someone like Tyler Hobden, even if you don't actually take part in the crime yourself.'

Baxter shook his head once again, only this time he laughed dryly. 'You would make a good preacher, Sam,' he declared easily. 'But believe me, I'll be able to live with my conscience quite easily, and this money will help me if it ever does start to trouble me.'

'Do you think you are the only person who has ever been hurt by their fellow man?' Sam asked. 'Bob Ward's wife was killed by his neighbour's sons, and he killed them both for it – but he also faced up to the fact that he had broken the law and had to stand trial, and then he went on living without being bitter about it for the rest of his life.'

'Damn the law. I only answer to my law, and that is to look after number one – Duke

Baxter,' the deputy growled.

'If you think that you're beyond the law that every other person has to live by, then you'll have to answer to my law – Brady's Law,' Sam answered coolly.

'You're a damn fool if you think you can take me, Sam,' Baxter warned as he un-pinned his deputy's badge and tossed it across the floor towards the youngster. 'You can have that piece of tin as I won't need it any more. I'm going to leave this place now and these saddle-bags are going with me.'

Sam's mind was already made up, and he was determined to stop Baxter from leaving. He knew that the deputy had been faster to the draw the last time they had faced each other, but that time they had only been playing about. He felt calm and relaxed and had no fear of death, and inside really believed that he could beat Baxter.

'You're not leaving,' he declared simply. 'I'm taking you back to Logan to face trial. So if you want to leave this place it is going to be over my dead body.'

'You're a damn idiot, Sam,' Baxter growled irritably. 'I always thought you were an intelligent young man, but you're proving yourself to be an idealistic fool.'

Sam ignored this comment and instead

watched the eyes of the deputy closely. 'Either put your gun on the table, or draw it – the choice is yours,' he demanded.

The deputy didn't hesitate and went for his six-gun, but Sam was ready for him and his hand plucked his six-gun from its holster. His draw was fast and fluid, but Baxter was faster. It all happened in a split-second, but to Sam it seemed like an eternity as the words 'Keep calm and keep drawing' passed through his mind. Even when he saw the muzzle-flash of Baxter's six-gun and felt the impact of the bullet in his chest, he continued to level his own weapon and fire. His six-gun fired a split-second after that of Baxter's, but this didn't register in his brain as pain spread through his chest and made his arms feel like lead. He could no longer hold the weight of his six-gun, and it slipped from his fingers to crash noisily to the floor. Slowly his legs buckled under him, and he fell to the floor as everything faded away into darkness.

SEVENTEEN

A girl's voice called out Sam's name. He attempted to open his eyes to see who it was but the light was much too bright for him, so he closed them again. He wasn't sure where he was, but he felt comfortable and at ease.

Once again the voice called out his name, only this time he recognized it. It belonged to Sarah Sainsbury, and her gentle reassurances convinced him to try to open his eyes once again. He looked straight up into her angelic face, and the light no longer bothered him because her head was blocking it from his view.

'Where am I?' he asked.

'You're safe with me,' she replied with a loving smile on her face as she gently stroked his brow.

'I was shot,' he stated, and made to sit up, but she stopped him with her hand in the middle of his chest.

'I told you that you're safe,' she insisted gently as she once again began to stroke his brow. 'And I want to thank you for avenging my father's murder.'

'I didn't get to Hobden, someone else killed

him,' he replied honestly, and then suddenly realized that his old companion wasn't anywhere to be seen. 'Where is Tate?'

'He's coming,' she replied. 'And when he gets here I must leave.'

A feeling of desperation gripped Sam as these words sank in, and he tried to sit up once again only to be pushed back down onto his back by the young girl. 'Why do you have to leave?' he asked her. 'Stay with me, please.'

'I can't stay, Sam,' she replied sadly. 'I've got to go, but I'll always remember what you did for me.'

'But I love you, Sarah,' he declared. 'I want to look after you for the rest of our lives.'

'And I love you, Sam, and I'll always be with you while you carry that watch,' she replied, before bending forward and kissing him on the lips. 'But I must go now because your friend Tate is coming, and he will look after you.'

'I don't need Tate to look after me. I want you,' the young bounty-hunter insisted, and once again tried to sit up, but he found that even though the girl had climbed to her feet and was walking away from him, he could feel the pressure of her hand on his chest and it was holding him down on his back.

'Don't leave me, Sarah,' he begged her but she was already walking away into the mist that *swirled around them both. She stopped momentarily to wave to him sadly, before then disappearing from sight into the mist.*

'Sarah – don't leave,' he shouted after her, but she was already gone.

'Are you okay, Sam?' an anxious voice asked the young bounty-hunter, but the tears that welled in his eyes made it hard to focus on the person speaking. He suddenly remembered who the voice belonged to and blinked the tears from his eyes to clear his vision.

'Tate?' Sam inquired as he focused on his old companion, who was kneeling beside him on the floor. The room where he was lying slowly came into focus, and Sam recognized it as the room where he'd had the gunfight with Duke Baxter.

'What's wrong with you, youngster?' Tate asked with concern plain in his voice.

'I've been shot in the chest,' Sam informed his old partner. 'Is it bad?'

'I can't see any blood,' the old bounty-hunter informed him as he checked the youngster's clothing, but all he found was a tear in the left pocket of Sam's shirt.

Tate reached out and pulled the silver half-hunter watch from the youngster's pocket, and saw a dent in the outer casing. He instantly realized that the watch had deflected a bullet away from Sam's heart, and that this had saved his life. 'You're a lucky young man,' he told him. 'I'd say you've probably got a cracked rib or two, but this watch has suffered a lot more damage than you have.'

Sam felt a wave of relief flood through his body, and tried to sit up, but the pain that grabbed at his chest forced him to give up his attempt.

'Did Hobden do this to you?' Tate asked, but before Sam could answer, Bob Ward knelt down beside them.

'Baxter is dead,' the farmer announced. 'He's been shot clean through the heart.'

'What's been going on around here, Sam?' Tate asked. 'Duke was supposed to wait until we arrived before coming in here after Hobden.'

'Help me up off this floor and I'll tell you all about it,' Sam offered as he struggled to sit up. This time, with the help of his two companions, he managed to climb to his feet and move across to sit at one of the tables.

'Duke Baxter was in with Hobden,' he informed them, and received a look of doubt in return from both men. 'He set the Mitchell Wells bank job up with Hobden, and then came here to collect his share of the money. But I guess he'd decided to take all the money and remove the only people who knew that he was a crook while he was at it – so he killed Hobden and Dixan before they could expose him.'

'But who shot you, and who killed Baxter?' Tate asked.

'Baxter shot me in a gunfight after I told him that I wasn't going to let him get away, and that I was going to take him back to Mitchell Wells to face the courts,' Sam informed his old partner. 'And I guess I must have shot him after he had already hit me in the chest.'

Both Tate and Bob shook their heads in disbelief at what they had just heard. Neither of them had suspected Baxter of being involved with Tyler Hobden, but now it all began to make sense. He had been keen on giving up the chase on Hobden back in Logan, and when that plan had failed he had insisted on riding in to the outlaws' camp alone to give him time to take out Hobden and Dixan before they could incriminate him.

'You're a very lucky man,' Bob Ward informed Sam as he accompanied Tate over to examine the two dead outlaws' bodies. 'He was damn fast with that six-gun by the sound of it.'

'The fastest,' Sam replied simply, and he looked at the damaged pocket-watch that he was still holding in his right hand. He remembered the dream that he'd had while unconscious on the floor, and he suddenly felt an overwhelming urge to climb onto his horse and hurry back to Mitchell Wells. He attempted to stand up but a pain in his chest stopped him in his tracks, and he sat back down on his chair after giving out a groan of agony.

'What the hell do you think you're up to, Sam?' Tate admonished him. 'You've probably got a couple of cracked ribs there, so sit still until we get the chance to help you over to your bed.'

Sam did as he was told and realized now that he was in no fit condition to carry out a long ride back to Mitchell Wells. He felt annoyed by the restrictive injury, but also realized that a couple of cracked ribs was a cheap price to pay when it could well have been a bullet through his heart.

Finally the two older men moved across to help him to his feet, and they headed for the door. The young bounty-hunter groaned from the pain that came from his injured ribs, but he gritted his teeth and continued on out of the building. He was soon lying comfortably on his bunk, and Tate set about strapping his chest with a tight-fitting bandage made from an old bed-sheet. There was a bruise already forming on Sam's chest where the watch had been forced against his body by the impact of the bullet, and Tate predicted that he would have a large black mark there by morning.

The old bounty-hunter sat on the side of the youngster's bunk and shook his head sadly. 'I'm sorry that I let you down, Sam,' he apologized. 'I should've realized what Duke Baxter was up to well before now – and I damn near got you killed by my slow-wittedness.'

'You're not to blame, Tate,' Sam assured him. 'He was a nice guy, and had me completely fooled too. I don't think he really wanted to hurt me; in fact I think he even tried to protect me from Hobden and his men, but I forced him to draw on me when I wouldn't let him leave with the money. So, I guess he wasn't quite as bad as Hobden, but there was only a fine line between them.'

Tate sat and considered this reply for some

time before speaking again. 'You would be wise to let everyone think that it was Hobden who killed Baxter,' he advised Sam. 'If it becomes known that you killed him in a fair gunfight, then every gun-happy kid around will be out to have a go at you to see if they can prove they're faster.'

'That's good advice,' Bob Ward assured the youngster. 'But I guess it's up to you whether you want to be known as the person who killed Duke Baxter?'

'I take no pride in the fact that I killed him,' Sam replied indignantly. 'Actually I was thinking that maybe we could keep his involvement with Hobden a secret, and then he would at least have an untainted reputation.'

'I think that's a good idea, Sam,' Tate agreed, and Bob Ward nodded his head as well. 'Now that we've settled that, I suggest you get some sleep while we go and make sure that all of Hobden's men are accounted for.'

EIGHTEEN

The pain in Sam's chest felt like someone was sliding a hot knife in and out between his ribs, but he was determined not to let this show on his face as he pushed his mount along at an easy canter beside Tate Sharp and Bob Ward. They were about a mile from the Wards' farmhouse where they had left Sarah Sainsbury some seven days before, and Sam was excited at the thought of seeing her again.

This was their fourth day on the trail since Sam and his companions had left the outlaws' camp, and he was feeling sore and weary. They had managed to make it back to the town of Logan the day after the shoot-out at the Red Hills camp, and had spent a further night in the town to rest up after handing over the bodies of Tyler Hobden and his men to the new sheriff – and to bury Duke Baxter. The deputy's funeral had been a small affair that was only attended by the three men and a tearful Kate Brown – who was deeply saddened by the deputy's death.

The next day they had headed on for Mitchell Wells, but Tate had insisted that they take their time and make camp for two more nights on the way.

They reached Mitchell Wells around noon, and had given the local sheriff the news about his deputy's death. The sheriff had merely shaken his head sadly on hearing this news, and made the cryptic comment of 'Maybe it was for the best' before thanking all three men for returning the bank's money, and then handing over the reward to them for doing so.

Sam's impatience had threatened to overpower him as he was forced to wait for Tate and Bob to finish their business with the sheriff, but he managed to suppress his eagerness until they finally started out of town on the last leg of their journey to the farm. The closer they got to the farmhouse, the more excited the young bounty-hunter became, but he forced himself to remain calm.

When Bob Ward's house finally came into view, Sam could no longer hold back his excitement, and spurred his horse into a gallop to cover the final hundred yards. He felt a surge of emotion in his chest as he thought of the beautiful young girl waiting at the farmhouse, and no longer noticed the pain from his cracked ribs as he quickly closed in on his destination. His two companions also sped up their mounts to keep up with him, and the three men finally drew to a halt outside the house.

Sam was the first to slide down from his horse and head for the front door. He was within ten feet of it when Hope Ward stepped out through the doorway and blocked his entry. Sam smiled on seeing her, but his smile froze when he saw her face.

'Where's Sarah?' he asked.

'She's not in there, Sam,' she revealed hesitantly.

'Then where is she?' he asked in a strained voice.

'She died four days ago,' Hope replied sadly and held out her hands to him.

'No – you're lying!' he accused her, and pushed past her into the house before making directly for the bedroom where he had last seen Sarah. He entered the room to find the bed empty, and there was no sign that she had ever been there in the first place.

'Sarah!' he cried out at the top of his voice, before turning and running back through the house to the front door where Tate and

Bob were now standing with Hope.

'Where is she?' he demanded loudly in a voice that was edged with insanity. 'What have you done with her? I want to know where she is!'

Suddenly Bob Ward loomed in front of him, and the last thing the youngster remembered was the impact of the farmer's fist against his chin, before the world faded away into total darkness.

Tate Sharp crossed from the house towards the stand of trees where the two graves were clearly marked with white crosses. Each cross bore the name of the person who was buried beneath, and next to the one that read 'Sarah Sainsbury', Sam sat quietly. They had been back at the farm three days now, and every one of those days Sam had spent sitting next to the girl's grave. He had come in for meals and to sleep, but the rest of the daylight hours were spent at her graveside. Tate had left him alone to handle his own mourning, but he now felt that it was time he intervened.

'How are your ribs today, Sam?' the old bounty-hunter asked as he sat down next to the younger man at the graveside.

Sam looked around at his old companion

and for a moment seemed not to have heard the question. Finally he smiled at Tate and answered. 'I'd forgotten all about them to tell you the truth. I guess I've been a bit too preoccupied the last few days to even think about them.'

'You seem to have finally come to terms with Sarah's death?' Tate observed.

'You might say that,' Sam replied sadly. 'But I'll never forget her as long as I live.'

'That's not a bad thing either, Sam,' Tate concluded. 'She was a special person who didn't deserve to experience what she did, but I think she was happy to have met you before she died.'

Sam didn't reply to this, but instead looked back down at the grave. He took a deep breath before turning back to face his old companion. 'Did Hope happen to tell you when Sarah actually died?'

'Yes – it was the night we were at the outlaws' camp in the Red Hills,' Tate informed him. 'Sarah was suffering from a bad fever and was delirious. She was talking out loud to her dead father, and then she called out your name and was talking to you – just after that she passed away.'

A smile creased Sam's face as he remembered the dream he'd had while unconscious on the floor of the outlaws' cabin after being shot by Duke Baxter. He wasn't normally a superstitious person, but he now believed that Sarah had really spoken to him on that night – but he kept this to himself.

'I've got something here for you,' Tate announced, and passed a pencil and some paper across to the youngster.

'You told me you had promised her that you would write to your parents as soon as you got back and I think you should keep that promise.'

Sam took the items from his old companion and nodded his head in acknowledgement of this request. He smiled to himself and knew that Tate had finally won the argument over him writing to his parents, but he was happy to give in to his advice.

Tate then climbed to his feet and walked away towards the house. He stopped momentarily to look back at his young companion, and smiled when he heard Sam talking out loud to himself as he wrote on the paper with the pencil. He then continued on towards the house and left Sam to his writing.

'Dear Ma, Pa, Luke and Sarah. I guess it's been a long time since you last saw me, so I thought I had better write to let you know that I'm okay. I have this very good friend called Tate Sharp, who has been looking after me since I left home – although sometimes I think it's more like me looking after him...'

The publishers hope that this book has given you enjoyable reading. Large Print Books are especially designed to be as easy to see and hold as possible. If you wish a complete list of our books please ask at your local library or write directly to:

Dales Large Print Books
Magna House, Long Preston,
Skipton, North Yorkshire.
BD23 4ND

This Large Print Book for the partially sighted, who cannot read normal print, is published under the auspices of

THE ULVERSCROFT FOUNDATION

THE ULVERSCROFT FOUNDATION

... we hope that you have enjoyed this Large Print Book. Please think for a moment about those people who have worse eyesight problems than you ... and are unable to even read or enjoy Large Print, without great difficulty.

You can help them by sending a donation, large or small to:

The Ulverscroft Foundation, 1, The Green, Bradgate Road, Anstey, Leicestershire, LE7 7FU, England.
or request a copy of our brochure for more details.

The Foundation will use all your help to assist those people who are handicapped by various sight problems and need special attention.

Thank you very much for your help.